THE RAVEN SOUND
By Kit Derrick

ISBN   978-1-8384267-2-9

https://www.facebook.com/Hypnopub

Acknowledgements

I want to thank Alex Proyas, Sean Bonney, Charles Dickens and Liverpool, all of them helped inspire this story in the first place, whether they know it or not. I'm guessing not. The Liverpool History Society, Marilyn Monroe, Willy Russell, my vinyl and DVD collections, and Adrian Henri similarly helped prompt, stimulate or advance ideas, all definitely without their knowledge, but you've all been a great help guys!

Thanks go to Nick and Hayley for their sterling work as supporting artists in a critical scene. They blend in so well you wouldn't even know they were there. Credit must go to Belinda, Porky, Nick and sundry others for letting me bore them and bounce ideas off them at various points and to the wonders of the internet for providing source material.

I'd also like to thank my beta readers, Scott Rhine, and Ruby Bunce for the invaluable feedback and comments, which have made a huge difference and pointed me in a number of additional directions. I'd particularly like to thank Tony Barley, a quite shy man who has inspired so many over the years with his passion, and who provided me with invaluable feedback over the bits I really needed to revisit and rewrite (and I really did need to!)

Cover by BLUSH

Contents

ONE – 17th October 2024

"You have sixteen hours left to live, Jack. Quite probably less..."

And then he fucking grinned at me, as though this was a good thing to hear.

It wasn't exactly what I'd been expecting.

TWO – 17th October 1994

I blinked.

And blinked a second time, disoriented.

The first thing I become conscious of is brightness, the second is the impression that my immediate surroundings are a vibrant green, and the third... that it's fucking cold. Excuse the language, I suppose I should be better behaved at my age but I am what I am.

I shiver involuntarily and shake my head quickly from side to side. The latter movement is deliberate and voluntary, to try and snap myself back to full awareness. I don't know why I bother as the only outcome is a painful twinge in my neck, adding physical discomfort to my sense of mental dislocation.

A raindrop hits me square on the nose, and this is the event which jolts me into opening my eyes wider and properly looking around, which I'll admit is a more practical method of discovering where I am. At the same instant I realise that I'm very disturbingly sober, and definitely not in The Caledonia any more.

Do you know how sometimes your existence can seem a little unreal? I'm thinking of the immediate aftermath of a drinking session, but before you've fully fallen asleep. Do you know that feeling? When you haven't quite reached the stage of being hungover, but at the same time you know you're beyond the stage where you feel like you're drunk? Time itself is bewildering, you're not entirely sure what has recently happened, what's real and what isn't, not even certain if you're actually awake or if you might already be dreaming. You don't feel as though anything bad is happening, but also haven't much in the way of a clue what the hell is going on. If that makes any sense to you, then you'll understand my basic mindset at this exact moment. But multiplied many times over.

If you don't understand what I mean, try taking one wrap of speed, drink two large whiskies, smoke a joint, ask someone to blindfold you, put you in a car and drop you off somewhere, then spin you round ten times, rip off the blindfold and disappear. You may be slightly disoriented, nauseous, unsteady on your feet, and find the words "what the fuck" screaming themselves at your conscious brain. That's where I'm at right now.

Physically, I'm sitting on a park bench. That much I've discovered. It's daylight, afternoon I assume (not sure why I assume this but it seems afternoon-ey), and a quick scan around brings the tall shadow of the Huskisson Memorial into view. I cling onto that image, blinking at it several times to make sure it stays firmly put, as if my eyelids are shutters which can control reality. The memorial is a fixed point I know, and I'm not letting that fucker go for anything until I work out what's going on. Or how I got here. It will stay squarely in my sights until I find at least one more thing that makes some sense.

Staring intently at the stonework I try to think back to the last thing I remember with any certainty, before that raindrop hit my nose. This proves to be harder than I expect. My memory is a jumble at the best of times, and I long since stopped worrying about that, as it isn't like anything much of note ever happens to me. Well, apart from the cancer and the heart attack. To be more precise, I should say that nothing much of note happens to me on a daily basis. My mind wanders off to try and identify some significant memory of my recent daily life which might explain my current situation. It then jumps randomly about through several of the more recent years, increasingly frantic that it doesn't find anything relevant, interesting, or even worthy of note.

Another raindrop. Again, right on my nose. I only mention that as it is the event which brings my mind back to my present surroundings; how the fuck am I here in the daytime, on a park bench?

Caledonia. The Caledonia. The Cali. Like a container ship with a huge turning-circle, my thoughts gradually round to face in the appropriate direction and return my focus to the pub I should currently still be sitting in. I was there, what... moments ago? A day ago? A week ago? I stare even more intently at the Memorial, urging my memory to get a grip and focus. I'm clearly out of practice at either of those actions, as the next thought that follows is whether I can now add unexplained blackouts to my unimpressive CV.

I'd been in the pub. The twinkly man with the strange hat. Marilyn Monroe. Jameson whisky. All just fleeting images at the minute. I'm feeling light headed, the images are scattered and don't link up. Disjointed. My mouth is dry and my bloodstream is distinctly alcohol free, which I don't like at all. I stand up uncertainly, one hand on the back of my bench, wary, and briefly wondering if my legs will work. My eyes are still locked firmly on my one fixed point of reference as I run through a mental checklist.

Legs working as they should? – yes. Sense of balance? – no worse than usual. Risk eyes in a

6

different direction? – unsure if I should but willing to give it a shot if there's a chance it might help. I scan left and right quickly, taking in as much information as I can before returning my gaze to the safety of the monument. Yes, I'm in St James' cemetery. A public park by the cathedral. That explains the green, and the presence of the Huskisson Memorial itself should have given that much away really. A memorial to the first man run over by a train. Strange, the details that your brain retains, which in this instance is a detail fuck all use for explaining my current reality. I'm not too far from the place where I'd (be precise Jack, from where I *think* I'd) last been, and this is a slight comfort. Shouldn't be, it doesn't help a jot, but any crumb of reassurance is very welcome right now. Anything solid is reassuring. With that speck of sanity and comfort settling back into my foggy perception, I reach absently into my jacket for my phone.

I reach again, less absently and more urgently. And then search in the other pockets, though I always keep my phone in exactly the same location, so a part of me must already know it's gone. There's no sign of my wallet either. The parts of my brain not distracted by my location and sense of dislocation are working hard, trying to put together a scenario which might explain at least a part of what's currently happening. Options include, one; that I'd

7

been too hammered and lost or left them somewhere (which is unlikely as I tend to always keep hold of the essentials whatever the situation), or two; that I've been mugged, which, much as I loved my home city, isn't exactly beyond the realms of possibility... but I digress. Frequently. You should be aware of that before we start.

I sit down on the bench again, hands going up to my face to search for blood or swelling, or other signs of being attacked. I find none, as at the same time the seeds of possible explanations for my present situation become incrementally more coherent. I realise that signs of being attacked, such as blood or swelling, are also equally common from being so off your tits that you wake up in a strange place, remembering nothing, without your phone or wallet. So the discovery of an injury wouldn't have been helpful and checking had been a fairly pointless exercise. I carry on checking anyway, as there is no benefit in leaving something half done once you've started. It gives my brain sufficient space to recognise that I'm missing the big picture. I don't know how I got here or why I'm here. Here is also strangely empty. There are usually some dog walkers around, pretty much any time of the day.

At the very edge of hearing I think I detect a very faint whispered voice, a man's voice that is almost recognisable. I can't make out the exact words but they seem like they're trying to help me, telling me it's time to begin. I don't understand what that means and dismiss the suggestion. I don't know what I need to begin, only that I need to methodically examine everything I can if I'm going to discover the reason for this... oddness.

I thrust my hands deep into my jeans pockets, and my fingers hit a substantial amount of coins, which a quick manipulation, a chinking, then a more practical looking at, reveal to be pound coins. I don't remember having these. My current eyeline shows that I'm wearing what seems to be some sort of desert boot or brown suede shoe. I don't recall owning anything like those either, but I decide to shrug this off as something for later, and the least of my current pressing mysteries. The back of my mind twists my attempts at searching for answers, and points me back towards the word 'pub.'

I shrug for no particular audience, and stand. No benefit in staying here, not now that I know where 'here' is, so it must be time for a new location. Perhaps not The Cali. Not yet. First, a short walk to blow the cobwebs and give my brain a chance to right itself, and then on to the pub. It's a sensible plan. A solid plan. Solid and sensible are something I can grasp onto, so I do.

I sigh and set off towards the slope of the path back up to civilisation and the road. There's something about the coins that bothers me, but I can't put my finger on it, and again, in the larger picture of this mystery, that specific detail isn't such a biggie. I have money which I can physically put my fingers on, even if I don't have a wallet or phone, and money is always useful. Ironically, the tune of Sandie Shaw singing 'Always Something There to Remind Me' pops into my thoughts. The mental image of a pint hovers at the back of everything.

#

I have to admit that I don't pay a huge amount of attention to my surroundings as I walk, a frown etched across my face. I suppose I must be vaguely aware of LIPA, the Paul McCartney 'Fame School', on my left, and very vaguely aware of crossing the road and walking past Gambia Terrace, a huge row of old Georgian buildings, but nothing I pass demands my focus. I'm not even aware of the subconscious itinerary I have of heading up to Falkner Square, and then looping back round the block towards the closest hostelry. The route isn't important and can take care of itself. It's a very short and familiar path to tread, long enough to be able to claim you've 'had a walk' without being far enough to be tiring, risk getting lost, or to delay the necessary acquiring of alcohol. Things always appear to make more sense with a drink inside you.

I'm not claiming alcohol allows improved logic, decision making or insight, but you care a little less. It's accepting the 'appear to make sense' element which is the key part to the success of my approach. With alcohol inside, you can blank out the bits of reality you don't like, or don't understand, more easily. The elements that remain, the more palatable ones, then 'appear' to make more sense. I find it to be a sound philosophy.

I undertake a mental inventory as I walk, as the best starting point must surely be to confirm what I know for certain first, and to then move on to the things I don't know. I'm staring down at the pavement as I walk, the better to avoid dogshit, so the logical approach is for me to start my inventory from the feet up.

Unfamiliar boots, though comfortable, and by now I've determined they are definitely boots rather than shoes. Ankle high desert boots, like you used to get in the Army and Navy Stores, back when they still existed. Next up, a pair of jeans, which adds nothing useful to my knowledge. Twenty separate one pound coins (I've counted three times to be certain); surprising, but in a good way. No keys.

Troubling, but we can leave that for later and file along with missing wallet and phone.

I have on a quite comfortable, and well-fitting check shirt which seems to be vaguely recognizable but, as sartorially challenged as I am, I just tend to grab whatever shirt I find in the flat so long as its relatively clean, and rarely pay attention to a specific pattern or colour. This one is grey/blue, which seems feasible for me to own, quite inoffensive and unremarkable. Half like me then. Over this shirt, I'm sporting a rather perplexing brown leather jacket. Not that surprising in itself, I'll grant you, as I quite often wear a brown leather jacket, just... not this one. A brief arm stretch shows it fits me well enough, and I couldn't really say what seems off with it beyond an aura of 'very slight wrongness'. As I mentioned, I'm not the most attentive person when it comes to my own clothes, and the jacket is certainly appropriate for me, and the type of thing I would wear; lots of pockets filled with items that looked like they might be mine; some tissues and loose humbugs, a Bic Biro, sunglasses that had no doubt been there for a few years, regardless of the weather. So it isn't anything about my jacket that disturbs me, it's just that I don't remember actually owning this specific one at all. This realisation fits in with my other experiences of the previous five minutes. I can't put my finger on a single thing that is particularly bizarre or out of place, nothing that individually causes too much concern in and of itself, beyond the fact that several observations and items I carry or wear just don't seem quite 'right'. Under my breath I'm humming 'Bits and Pieces' by the Dave Clarke Five, though I'm not sure why. I don't even like that song.

The biggest enigma, of course, is why I opened my eyes sitting on a park bench, with apparent short-term memory loss. And there's a big something missing from before that too. I'm sure there's a conversation I should be remembering, an important one that would shed some light on, well, everything. I have a sense I should know why I'm here, but nothing beyond that vague sense. Solve these little conundrums, and I assume the current minor inventory details I'm going through will also start to make sense. I'm quite logical when I want to be, or at least able to reason things through step by step; logical might be over-claiming.

"Stop prevaricating Jack... remember the butterfly..." The voice is distinct this time, a light, whispered male voice but there is no-one else in sight. This is a new and peculiar development, and I'm uncertain if it's just my imagination. As it makes no sense and doesn't help me to discover anything useful, I choose to ignore the words. I have enough to focus on as it is, and logic dictates that the absence of a speaker means it isn't real.

You might expect that I'd be a little freaked out by the recent turn of events, and a disembodied voice, but I'm not the sort of person to be easily freaked out. I've lived long enough, and through enough different life events that very little takes me by surprise or shocks me any more, and to be perfectly honest, the drive and curiosity I had when I was young has also long since gone the way of my hairline. I can count the things that really matter to me on my fingers, and still have nine or ten to spare. If you don't care to begin with, it's hard to care when something unexpected happens. As a creature of habit I can still feel uncomfortable at change, but it would take more than this to make me properly worry.

The first full, logical (okay, reasonably logical) conclusion that comes to mind as I amble along the pavement is that somewhere in my lost (hours, days, weeks?) I've inexplicably been clothes and shoes shopping. This seems fairly unlikely, I'll grant you. And what I'm currently wearing is... let's just call it 'worn in,' shall we? The conclusion of a sudden decision for a shopping trip for a new wardrobe of shop-fresh items doesn't match up to my current experience. I tweak the theory slightly, to remove the clothes being new. Charity shopping isn't beyond me, true, but I'm comfortable enough financially to buy new if I need to (in other words if something wears out or gets damaged), so the possibility that I'd recklessly decided to suddenly kit myself out in Oxfam leftovers can also be relegated to the lower tier of likelihood. What I'm wearing does have a familiar (lack of) style though, and they seem like they *could* be my own clothes, and in the absence of another explanation for my outfit, this proves vaguely, if nonsensically, comforting.

A very fleeting passing whim skims over my conscious train of thought, about the possibility of aliens; kindly aliens who abduct you, strip you, probe or whatever they do to get them off, keep my original clothes as a souvenir but with their high-tech machines create a passable alternate ensemble to send me home in. Possibly out of space mushrooms. As you might guess, this passing thought passes without me paying it too much attention. It isn't a very probable explanation either. Even so, I briefly consider putting my hand down the back of my jeans to check for evidence of probing. I resist. It might look a bit odd in the middle of the street. Instead, I try once more to re-assemble what I know of my last coherent and definite memory.

This causes an unpleasant prickling sensation at the back of my neck, as though something important is swimming tantalisingly out of reach. Something important and not very palatable. I try shifting my train of thought back even earlier in the evening in search of an anchor to work from. I know I'd been quite drunk before arriving at the pub tonight, that much was definite. I was later than usual setting off to The Cali, after an annoying phone conversation with Shelly. Yes. This is something solid I'm sure of. Solid is very good. I curse, as my boot splashes into a puddle in the cracked paving stones, and I shake my leg ineffectually, wondering why anyone would deliberately choose suede desert boots, and grateful it was rainwater and not dogshit I stepped in. So it had been raining earlier then. Another fact. I add it to my slim dossier.

It's been over fifteen years since my divorce, and all the subsequent conversations with Shelly annoyed me. Come to think of it, pretty much every conversation I've ever had with her has been annoying, full stop. Which partly explains the divorce, from my side anyway. For the life of me I can't remember what I'd been annoyed about this time, or why she'd phoned me. I have an inkling that terming myself 'annoyed' might be an understatement. 'Royally pissed off' might be closer to the mark. If her intention had been to make me start drinking whisky earlier at home and to lose track of time, then it had worked. One rational part of my brain relents enough to admit that this alone was an unlikely reason for her to have called, but I dismiss that part of the evening again for now, as Shelly doesn't seem relevant to what is currently going on. Whatever had happened to me and caused my present perplexing location and attire, it had happened much later in the evening than the phone call.

I silently recount to myself, step by step, the details which I can remember and which I'm certain are correct. I'd walked to the pub by my usual route, and had been feeling fractionally better as it came into view. The Cali wasn't exactly a refuge but it was consoling, like chicken soup or 'It's a Wonderful Life' on the TV on a cold winter's Sunday afternoon. I'd ordered my usual pint of bitter and a whisky chaser and had taken up residence in my regular place by the table towards the back wall. Straight away, something hadn't seemed right. I remember now. Some people think that change is good. Cunts. It isn't.

Someone had changed the pictures on the back wall of the pub, and in the centre, over the bricked-up fireplace, there now hung a framed print of a depressed-looking Marilyn Monroe in a sequinned dress, hand on face, staring vacantly towards the bar. Actually, as more details come back to me, I recall that her eyes seemed to look in slightly different directions, one at the bar and one off towards the toilets. It hadn't helped my still dour mood. There used to be a bank of washing machines on that back wall at one point. The failed 'laundropub' phase of The Cali. I'd liked that. Ridiculous idea, but it had appealed to me. When you've been drinking, there's something strangely entrancing about watching the drum of a washing machine tumble and spin. You can watch it for hours. Trust me, that isn't conjecture. I know.

Anyway, I'd sat there staring at this fucking picture. I can't remember what it had directly replaced but I must have liked it more, as my already gloomy mood had taken a distinct turn for the worse staring at her face. The pub had lifted my spirits for exactly four minutes before providing something to piss me back off. Yes, hang on to that. That had happened. Another solid fact. At this rate of discovery, I'll have the answers I need before I finish my 'walk' and the pint that awaits me can be celebratory. The wind seems to whisper another word to me, in a different voice. The word is accusatory. The word is "arsehole." I ignore my auditory hallucination.

I kick through a pile of leaves just because they're there, taunting me with their knowledge of how they got to be on that pavement. There are a lot of leaves this year it seems. I head into the garden square to give my head just a fraction more time to straighten itself. When Liverpool had started to take off at the beginning of the nineteenth century the council, or whatever they were called then, had decided that in order to be taken seriously, they needed to ape London, had changed road names, and had built a number of garden squares to try to rival Bloomsbury and Russel Square and the like. It had never really taken off, but did leave the city with a few nice and unexpected green areas which survived the years and later became public parks for dogwalkers and junkies alike. This one was Falkner Square, one of the least successful, built just a little too late and just a little in the wrong spot. I know all this because I read an article about it in the Echo. I collect knowledge. You never know when it might come in useful. Don't judge a book by its cover, I may not have much of a formal education but that doesn't mean I'm not well read or knowledgeable about many subjects. The history of my city is one of them. The park itself is nice enough, if you like that kind of thing.

As I walk round the gravel path I get the feeling I'm being watched, though no-one is here and I'm the sole occupant. Until a figure with an oak walking stick limps through one of the gates and stops in front of me, that is, blocking the pathway. He's squinting at me slightly. I don't know him, but the way he looks at me suggests that he thinks he might know me. I'm no great judge but he's probably about my age, black, with quite shiny skin, he probably moisturises, has a neatly trimmed white beard and hair, is quite sharply dressed and has patent leather shoes so not short of a few quid. I'm pretty sure I haven't seen him before or I'd recognise him. He's quite distinctive.

"I know you, don't I?"

I push my lip out and raise my shoulders in a mummer's show of ignorance to indicate that I have no idea. He squints again, and I notice there's something wrong with his left eye.

"No, you can't be... sorry..."

He turns and limps back out of sight. Odd. I can't help shivering. Now that I've stopped walking, I'm at the mercy of the chilly wind so I pull my jacket tightly closed and zip it up to the neck. Back to my rediscovery of pertinent facts and my search for truth. In the absence of my mobile phone, I have no idea what specific time it is, but it has that retirement home feel of a late afternoon, and a glance up to the sky confirms the October dusk hovering on the verge of creeping in. Yes, I can be a poetic bastard when I want to be. I like poetry, I couldn't recite you any but I know what I like, and some of what I like is poetry.

A black cab roars past. I haven't seen much in the way of traffic since I left the cemetery, or any other people actually, apart from the strange limping man. I don't mind being alone in the usual course of events, but the solitude is unsettling today when I'm craving some normality.

The University campus is up ahead so that means there are bound to be people. More specifically, it means there are bound to be girl's arses, which makes it a double win. I like the fashion which has taken hold in the past few years for girls to wear leggings, or whatever you called them at the minute. Basically thick tights with no skirts or trousers, even this chilly time of year. I might be 60 and three times their age, but I can still enjoy the view. That's poetry too. It doesn't have to be a verse written down for a beauty to affect me.

You can't say that these days of course, have to pretend not to notice. We're quite Victorian in our attitudes when I come to think of it. So long as you don't say anything wrong out loud, and no-one admits to anything distasteful in the wrong company, you can pretty much do what you like. I start walking again, my pace a little faster. Like I say, I sometimes get easily distracted, and was starting to feel a little depressed by everything else, but admiring pert buttocks is a certified way of improving my mood, and regardless of the weather,

21

this new fashion is wonderfully common. I have no alcohol inside me yet, I'm cold and I have no real idea what the fuck is going on today, so the high probability of nearby girl's arses is a concrete step towards improving my mood. The journey of a thousand miles starts with a single peachy arse. Or something like that. I'll concede that universities aren't all bad.

#

I stop on the corner quite suddenly - the way you sometimes read about but don't ever imagine actually doing yourself. It makes me rock unexpectedly, and I blink eight or nine times. And then a couple more for good measure, wondering if my search for memories has taken me back too far, and is currently kicking me in the eyeballs to jolt me back to a form of reality. There, in front of me, is a car park. And to my right, a distance away, is the old stone church, the gym. Both are in daylight and unobstructed by shadow. I know that doesn't sound strange to you, yet, but stay with me.

I frown, and look back behind me, the way I've just come, but all appears much the same as it should there, so I swivel round to face forwards once more. Where I'm standing, I seem to be on a reality threshold. If all was right in the World, there should be more buildings in front of me right now. Big, ugly bastards of buildings, and quite a few of them. There should be a coffee shop next to me on the right. There should be a ubiquitous Tesco to my left. There shouldn't be a car park, and I shouldn't be able to see a church that no longer exists. Nothing is where I expect it to be.

Cars drive past, more of them now. They seem slightly... incorrect. My sensation of unreality goes up a notch. I stare up and down the street, aware that I'm still scowling, like this might force the World to notice and make amends. I'm just like that, my face automatically reflects my mood, I can't help it. It's why I never play poker. Any more.

I let the frown remain in place, not understanding what I'm looking at, and my brain has an internal battle. Yes, everything I can see is in the right location, but not for 2024. Everything is like I remember it used to be years ago, but shouldn't still be, not any more. I just stand and let the confusion wash over me for a moment. I'm distantly aware of the light drizzle that starts to fall.

In the absence of the view before my eyes starting to make more sense, my brain takes the decision to just go with it for now. If everything is as it seems, the car park, the church, the buildings as they used to be years ago, then The Carousel pub and beer should still exist, and also be mere footsteps away to my left. And beer is solid. Beer is good. Beer is reality and helps situations seem as if they make sense.

It is with great relief that this existence is at least consistent, and has the pub and therefore beer where it should be. I take the few required steps and I'm standing in the porch of The Carousel, seeing the poster blu-tacked to the wall on the way in, informing about the weekly meeting of 'The Black Elders'. This makes me smile a warm and genuine smile, though I know the sign used to make me feel distinctly uneasy at times. I'm a child of the sixties, and the change to a more politically correct world has been a bit of a struggle occasionally, working my way through the eighties and nineties, and the minefield of their changing sensibilities. Words that had previously been quite acceptable to use had started to cause offence faster than my ability to keep up.

It made no difference to my immediate social circle and my mates of course, but to others who didn't know us, Brian and Twelves had gradually become my 'black friends.' They'd always received descriptive nicknames, epithets (and insults) personally, but to many of the people I interacted with outside of our immediate community, the lads took on a new identity as those decades progressed. They became my 'black friends,' like that was a different thing. In some circles, primarily in the world of my work, it even morphed into a very bizarre badge of credibility. People I met who had been brought up away from cities, and in certain very Caucasian parts of Cheshire and Lancashire seemed to think it exotic that I 'mixed' socially with people of different skin tones. It's very odd looking back on that. Although the porch blocks and wind and separates me from any other people, I hear the first voice in my head once more, a seductive whisper.

"Take your time. You need to remember Jack... there's something important here." The voice doesn't scare me, or the fact I think I can physically hear the words, and I imagine it's my subconscious guiding me. The last half hour has been peculiar, and hearing myself think, while unusual, doesn't seem too out of the ordinary.

That sign in front of me in the porch reminds me of two very different experiences. The first, we must have been about early twenties, was in this very pub one night, with Brian a little the worse for wear after an afternoon's drinking. More than a little if I'm honest; even when he was pissed, Brian wasn't usually the sort to cause a scene. It had been out of character, but there had been some sort of evangelical Yank in the bar, invited by the Elders to talk about his involvement with civil rights. He'd been loudly espousing black power and community, and explaining how things were changing in the States, and how they would here too; how the Black Community would rise up and regain respect and the status they deserved. And as he'd paused for breath, Brian had stood, a little unevenly it has to be said, loudly butting in "Oh... shut the fuck UP!"

He'd launched right into a rant of his own, surprising me with the power and urgency of his speech, in retrospect something that must have been bubbling inside for some time. He challenged and jabbed his finger at the shell-shocked American, accusing him of talking a crock of shit (lovely phrasing), and accusing him of not knowing what he was talking about with regard to Liverpool. Wobbling slightly, Brian had started shouting that there wasn't a "fucking black culture", there was a "fucking Tokky (meaning Toxteth) community," but that the Somalis, West Indians and "all the others" (I never claimed he'd made total sense), had "fuck all in common" for a start, and even less in common with American cunts like him. I'd known that Brian didn't like Americans, though I never got to the bottom of why, but I'd sat open mouthed as he'd rounded on the closest of the elders, something I'd never seen him do before or after, and this had been more shocking than any of the words he spoke. His finger had jabbed at several individuals, on a crusade now, asking if there was one Black

Community, why couldn't they stop the Somalis and Nigerians in their fighting? I think that was the closest hint to whatever it was that bothered him so much. It wasn't the families that had grown up here that were the problem, but there had been elements from Somali and Nigerian families, more recently arrived, that had been causing friction around Granby Street for a number of years. It might have even started with something as small as a family feud, I don't know, but the problems we had at that point were well known to all of us. Everyone took a pause at that question, some embarrassed our issues were being aired for an outsider, some, like me, just shocked the outburst happened at all. That Brian, a young man with, let's face it, no particular standing or position, would openly and drunkenly, accuse and insult his elders and betters.

"If you can't even sort that out, you got no right to say you represent any Black f... flaming culture..." That had been straight into the face of one of the most senior of the Elders, and maybe the stony gaze coming back, or the realisation he'd gone too far made him pause, and pull back from swearing in that last line like he'd clearly intended. However pissed he might be, that would have been too much.

It had been more than I'd ever heard Brian say on the subject of race. His own background wasn't from any of the larger Toxteth communities; his dad was originally from Mali I think, worked on the docks, and his mum was a black Scouser born and bred, but not from any of the influential family lines. His dad had disappeared well before we'd met, even though I'd know Brian since we were small kids. As far as I'd known, Brian had always just thought of himself as being a Scouser rather than associating himself with any subset or demographic.

I don't recall the next sequence of events exactly, but I don't think we got *physically* thrown out. I think the silence and rising tension in the pub were enough for us to get the message and swiftly leave of our own accord. I do remember heading to the chippy round the corner before I spoke, something eloquent along the lines of "... what the fuck...?" before we both collapsed into hysterics. "American cunt" had been his only response.

That's the first memory the sign on the wall brings back, and it's oddly a happy one, of a good night out. The second is closely related, and from a few short years after that evening. I'd been in Manchester, at some sort of work event, part of my very short-lived early career repairing computers. I can't remember when it had been exactly, maybe 1988, and I've no idea how the subject had come up, but as I remember it now, I'd been part of a particularly all-white crowd in the bar after a seminar, and I'd told the story about Brian's outburst and the shellshocked reaction it received in order to ingratiate myself, the point of the retelling, to impress them that we'd been thrown out (I may even have embellished and said we were barred for life.) It hadn't occurred to me to tell it any differently than we usually did in the pub with the lads, so the story began with how Bri had challenged the 'Black Elders' and their 'Black Panther' friend (I don't think he was, but I'd added a few details over the years to spice the story up), showing how brave and daring we were. I'd laughed, expecting them to join in and think I was a great guy, challenging authority, getting kicked out of pubs, how I was 'one of the lads'.

I'll admit that I wasn't suited to that job or that crowd, and had judged my audience badly. The job lasted about another week until I gave up and went back to dealing. But I still remember telling that story as clear as anything. I don't think I've ever felt so uncomfortable, as it was made very clear to my quite surprised face that I was a racist for using "stereotype terms" (I remember that exact phrase). And they, I'm almost certain, had actually physically closed ranks and turned their backs on me. Like in a playground. I'd stood there in shock, uncertain quite what I'd done wrong. That's how I remember it anyway.

My point, as I enter The Carousel now, is that for years afterwards, whenever I saw that sign by the door of the pub after the experience in Manchester, all I could think of was the reaction I'd got. Deep down, whenever I saw that sign, I couldn't stop automatically questioning myself; 'Am I actually racist?' I hadn't thought so until that point. I'll hold my hands up to never liking the Welsh or the French. Or the Japanese for some reason (though that was probably from something I read about the war), but that doesn't count. In all honesty, we probably all were racist in our own way back in those days. But it was only that particular time, with a group of all-white strangers accusing me and taking the moral high ground, that I actually felt for the first time like I might be a racist myself. Or maybe it had been me realising the changing times.

I'd walked into The Carousel while I was remembering all of this, and straight up to the bar on auto-pilot. I'd nodded to the girl behind the counter, cleaning glasses, though I can't say I'd recognised her. I didn't look behind me so had never noticed the shadow of a figure outside the glass of the door.

The barmaid doesn't look pleased to be disturbed and as I'm still distracted by memories of the sign outside, her expression takes me back to another long-forgotten look of disapproval I'd once received, years before I'd started to question my own level of prejudice.

It must have been the late seventies or early eighties, when we were barely out of our teens. Brian had this great idea I should black up to go to a party being held by a University student he fancied, pretend to be his brother, and we'd both feign ignorance if anyone questioned it. He was convinced it would be hilarious and help break the ice with University types. Brian's younger sister had pissed herself laughing at the idea, and his mum just told us we were being pathetic and to grow up, slapping Brian round the back of the head and giving me an icy stare. Mrs Touré tolerated me as I was Brian's mate and looked out for him, and on occasion would even seem to vaguely approve of me, but she also scared me shitless. She was not a warm woman and I would never dare to cross her. I'd hovered nervously until she'd left, at which point, egged on by a sister with a make-up bag, we'd done it anyway. We were both thrown out of the house party minutes after getting through the door, both being accused of being racists. That had just made us laugh all the more, and it hadn't even registered that I should take the accusation seriously. Right now, the expression on the face of the girl behind the bar is one of disgust at my very presence, like one of those students at the party had, the only difference being that the barmaid is black herself.

Something is different in the bar, something strange. I'm brought back to the reality of my present by the tentative sniff I take, and I screw up my face at the smell I find. It is not good. I breathe in again, and search around trying to place where it might emanate from. My eye goes from table to table, taking a full minute to realise that the vast majority of the drinkers have either cigarettes in hand or full ashtrays on their tables. I breathe in once more and it smells much better the third time around, now that I understand what it is. This is what pubs are supposed to smell like. And just like that, some of the tension I hadn't realised was present in my shoulders ebbs out of me. I feel more relaxed, and not just because I'm ordering a (surprisingly cheap, only £1.42) pint from the sullen barmaid, or because I'm separate from the weirdness of the changed streets outside. The Carousel was never a student pub, it was always for locals, and though there aren't any familiar faces I can see or recognise here, I feel safer. The smell of stale tobacco is the catalyst. It's wonderfully bitter, and it's effect is that I feel I'm back where I truly belong. This is what I hadn't even known I needed. I find a spot by the window and settle myself.

I have a packet of peanuts and a table by the quiz machine, with a pint of whatever had been on the pump (I hadn't even looked to see what it was, but it tastes sharp and hoppy) and I take one more deep breath of the fantastically stale atmosphere. I'm home. I still don't know what happened in the last few hours, but I'm remembering things that I haven't thought about in years. And they're good memories, even the unpleasant ones, of happier and easier times.

#

I sit and drink for five or ten minutes, just letting the pleasure of being wash over me, and forgetting everything but the beer and the peanuts. I highly recommend it for any occasion. But it isn't long before my thoughts find their way back to The Caledonia and the mystery of what happened there.

Looking back, I think I may well have vocally addressed an uncharitable comment towards the picture of Marilyn Monroe above the fireplace, quite loudly. Well, actually, I know that I definitely had. No-one had paid any attention as it wasn't that out of character for me and I was treated by the other regulars as part of the fixtures and fittings, so no-one had cared enough to wonder why I'd spoken. But in the five seconds or ten minutes since I'd sat down and had first noticed the photograph of Marilyn, I'd been blaming her for most of the bad things that happened in my life. Recounting her guilt to myself had allowed me to get a lot more blame in, a lot faster. The out-loud comment was just a generically misogynist insult I suspect. At that exact moment there'd been no-one else present and suitable to blame my life on, and Marilyn was just there, convenient. So I'd had to say something to let her know.

I don't think the allocation of blame had even the vaguest link to reality if I'm brutally honest with myself. Not only because Marilyn was long dead, or because I'd never met her. Even if neither of those facts came into play, then I don't think being carcinogenic was one of her no-doubt numerous talents. Nor was causing heart attacks, that I was aware of. Well, she might have done that, people were easily over-stimulated back in the fifties I imagine, but I think I can trace mine to other more probable causes. While she wasn't directly responsible for my divorce or subsequent failure in the relationship department, there was something about her that made Marilyn's guilt on that score more likely. It might have been her tits as I recall them. They were supposed to be a great asset, but they'd looked pretty unimpressive when she sat there posing for that photo, face like a wet weekend.

Yes. She'd probably reminded me of Shelly. That would explain why the picture had pissed me off so much. I could vaguely remember a similar moment across our kitchen table when I realised that what I was looking at didn't love me any more. And I didn't love it. I wonder how long before me she'd known that herself?

My mind is wandering off into flights of fancy, and I try to pull myself back to more important and pertinent matters; what had happened next? I'd been scowling at this picture, even realising my face was physically twisted with distaste and momentarily wondering what I looked like (as you can tell by now, I have a short attention span and am easily distracted by many thoughts.)

I'd been so distracted by Marilyn's breasts and thoughts of my ex-wife that I hadn't even noticed him sitting down at my table. Yes, that twat with the twinkly eyes and the peaked hat. A hat indoors, for fuck's sake? By then I'd been in the mood to insult someone who wasn't in a picture on a wall and he'd arrived just at the right time for that, but I had sufficient sobriety left to know that sartorial insults would not be very convincing coming from me, so I'd refrained from commenting on the hat. Men who live in Glass Onions and all that.

I'd opened my mouth to speak but the way he was settled into his chair, donkey jacket over the back, pint two thirds drunk... it was just possible he'd been there all along, and I'd sat down at his table without noticing. I recall that this realisation had pissed me off as well. Well, it was usually my table, so why would I look for who else might be sitting there? Just for a second, I'd felt a shiver of almost embarrassment at the fact I was feeling offended by this man's very presence, quite possibly having sat down at what he justifiably thought of as 'his' table, and having then insulted the wall out loud, like a nut job. I suspect that my feelings may have shown quite blatantly on my face because, with a blink of those twinkly little eyes, he'd asked if I minded him joining me, just a hint of amusement showing in his voice. I don't usually mind making a twat of myself when I've been drinking, but I was still aware I'd barely finished shouting an insult at the appearance of a photograph and, to be honest, I just couldn't be arsed making more of a scene. Instead, I'd decided to ignore his existence as much as I could, shrugged that I didn't care one way or another, then looked down at my drinks.

"She had an unhappy life, didn't she?"

I'd raised my eyes slowly to see him looking where I'd been aiming by anger, at the photograph, something approaching regret on his features. I didn't like his expression.

"Good job she's dead then, isn't it?"

His eyebrows had raised a little higher than was normal when I'd said that. It had made him look like a fat leprechaun. Yes, that mental image is there now, it's all coming back to me. With a nod at my own achievement of a fatuous smart arse comment, but a quick comeback one, I'd turned back in the direction of the main pub and away from him. I'd decided that I deserved another pint for that. There's a nagging doubt in my mind now though, something about his voice being familiar.

I'm jerked out of my reverie by the realisation someone is standing over the table in the present, and that he's squinting at me. It surprises me so much that I don't even have time to feel annoyed before he speaks.

"I'm sorry. I just had to be certain. I haven't been back here for so long and you're the first person I've seen that I thought I recognised, my apologies."

It's the man from the park again. He's very eloquent and I believe his explanation. I haven't seen anyone I recognised since I woke up either, so I have some sympathy for anyone looking for the familiar. Not enough to offer him a seat but enough to let him talk. He smiles a crooked smile.

"Derek... Derek Joseph..."

He doesn't extend a hand and leans on his stick, but watches me to try and see if I have any flash of recognition at the name. I don't. There seems to be a sadness behind his dark brown eyes at the fact I don't know him, and his frame sags marginally. I feel slightly guilty for disappointing him, and offer my own name in recompense.

"Jack. Just Jack…"

That clearly means nothing to him either. He smiles a brilliant smile, though it isn't entirely convincing.

"When you get to our age, it's easy to forget, eh? I haven't been here in decades. I've been living abroad."

He peers around the room as he talks and when he looks back, I see now there's definitely something very wrong with his left eye, which accounts for the squint. What should be white is a strange hue of yellow and it's disconcerting. I don't reply to his comment and he releases a deep breath.

"The mind plays tricks is all. You remind me of someone, my friend. Someone I met shortly before I left but…" He had very little of any accent, maybe a hint of the transatlantic. "I forget that was a long time ago. He must be dead by now. A relative, perhaps..?"

His fishing and waiting for a response is irritating, and I decide I don't trust this man, even though I know nothing about him. There's a little spark of hopefulness in his good eye that's quite pathetic, so I throw him a bone. Or more accurately, give a non-committal a shrug that yes, it's possible he once met a relative of mine. The man waits a little longer, then uncertainty crosses his face, and I think he realises he's acting strangely. His mouth pinches slightly. I don't think he's used to not getting his way, nor being viewed as an oddity, despite his eye. Almost as soon as the expression appears, it vanishes, to be replaced with a bland smile.

"Sorry for disturbing you..."

He limps away, leaning on the stick and not looking back, or anywhere as far as I can tell. He makes slow progress but I keep my eyes on him until the door swings shut behind his retreating form, and I know he's actually left. This day is very peculiar. And for some unknown reason I've taken against Derek Joseph, whatever his story is. I resolve to leave after finishing my drink, in case he comes back. The surly girl behind the bar is watching me with suspicion, and might have been watching the whole encounter. Her continuing expression of disapproval still reminds me of the girl at the party when I'd worn blackface. And from there to the group in Manchester who'd shunned me.

I find my imagination going back to reflect on various stages of my life, second guessing myself. I'm not immune to the guilt, real or otherwise, that accusations of racism provoke. Even accusations from dickheads I barely knew, thirty five years ago.

39

When they get a foothold into my obsessive nature, they're hard to shake off. Unlike the old man with the stick, who leaves my thoughts.

"You were going somewhere with your thoughts, I believe..?"

Yes, I had been, before that interlude. The voice in my head doesn't take me by surprise any more. Yes, I'm not blind or stupid. I know the abuse the lads I hung around with had received from some groups, some people, some cops, and some arseholes, and I know the way society had treated many of my friends and neighbours was 'different' (I knew it as well as anyone as white as me could do), but that was just the society that we all lived in back then. Life was unfair, you could linger on it, or you could get on with your life. We'd just got on with our lives. The colour of skin came second to the community. Fuck me, that sounds pretentious doesn't it? Let me try again.

I've never been a fighter, but whether with words or boots, you went against one of us, in our streets, you went against everyone. Didn't matter if you hated the bastard's guts, you looked after your own. And in our little area on the edge of Toxteth you could say what you liked to each other, take the piss about anything, skin colour included, and we did, both ways. Like family though. Insults were water off a duck's arse.

I always chuckle when I remember one particular happening on a night bus home. Well, I wasn't technically heading to my *own* home, but that's a different story. Some drunk students had been on the top deck at the front, hammered enough to not care about their Home Counties accent as they slagged off parts of our city and the difference to 'back home.' One equally drunken Scouse woman had been the first to chime in. "Oi... no-one talks about Liverpool like that, you fucking Cockney bitch... if you don't like it why don't you just fuck off home?" That had been the rallying call. Taken aback, the girls had physically shrunk down and tried to be silent, to make the interruption disappear by ignoring it. But several other voices in the front few rows had heard and had decided it would be fun to join in, comments increasing in vitriol and volume as no response was forthcoming. The student closest to the aisle, blonde, big earrings, expensive coat, pulled herself together enough to try and calm the situation with an attempt at an apology that no offence had been meant. Red rag to a bull. Even more calls for them to fuck off back to where they came from. Pleading from Blondie, and tears from her friend, clinging tight to her arm as the atmosphere switched so fast from drunken revelry

41

to seeming hatred. I'd been sat a few rows back, watching, amused, and satisfied the girls had pretty much brought it on themselves. Seeing there was no win for them, the students had roused themselves enough to try and leave, which seemed eminently sensible, and had endured a barrage of further insults to their patronage and femininity, and more than one sharp shove and an attempted hair grabbing before they'd made it to the stairs. The first voice that had begun the attack on them turned around, and I noted that she was far closer to middle-aged than her attempts at fashion suggested. A raw and raucous laugh had broken out, followed by cheers from the other passengers, probably for the victory and departure of the young girls, though the brassy Scouser had literally taken a bow as if the cheers had been for her personally.

"It might be a shithole, but it's our fucking shithole!" Another cheer. "Slags..."

Yes, no-one from outside gets to do that, comment on us and ours. Our local community was like a further layer of that attitude. No-one from outside our small group of streets could challenge a single one of us and get off free, but within our own group, you could say what you liked with immunity. Race wasn't an issue between us, it was all of us against the World. That's the rose-tinted view I have now anyway, and I'm certain how I saw it at the time.

I forget about the times one of us would get the shit kicked out of him just for how they looked, and that it was rarely the ones that looked like me. I'm not saying that there weren't occasions when any one of us might have deserved a kicking for how we acted or what we did, but Brian and Twelves and Mick... well, they got it for other reasons too.

Looking around The Carousel right now, at the predominantly black faces, I can't help feeling a little guilty again for just being white, but I try and shake that away. There's no benefit in wallowing in what I should have done differently thirty years ago, and I have my own problems to deal with today. Having a little mental holiday about growing up is all well and good, but now it's time for me to take stock, to think on one thing only, and try to re-assemble what has happened to me since the twat in the peaked hat.

"Yes..." That familiar whispered voice in my head again.

#

He'd been surprised and a little annoyed at my reaction to his comment on the possible futures of Marilyn, the man in the hat, and had been expecting his statement about her sad life to be a conversation starter, or evoke empathy I suppose. I'd run out of empathy in about 2005 and have never been that interested in pointless conversations so it didn't have the intended effect on me. It had been all silence for a few minutes, which had suited me fine, as all I'd wanted was to drink and wallow anyhow. I think I'd been a little bit secretly pleased that I'd pissed him off. There was something about the man that had bothered me. And the fact he didn't shut up for long only added to that.

"You're local aren't you, I think I've seen you in here before?"

It had been my turn to raise my eyebrows, in a wordless 'no-shit Sherlock' response. Aside from the fact I was, indeed, at this table several times a week so he would have seen me if he'd ever been in the Cali before, of course I was a local. This wasn't a tourism destination pub. I'd just known he was going to keep looking at me like that with expectant puppy dog eyes until I said something though. So I had.

"I haven't seen you."

It wasn't an Oscar Wilde level of wit, I know.

"Ah..."

Those fucking twinkling eyes again.

"I'm not from round here really... not usually..."

The line between enigmatic and a pain in the arse is thin. And he was some way over it.

"I'm going for a piss. Don't touch my drinks."

I don't know why I'd bothered telling him, beyond the hope it might mean he didn't follow, or might fuck off before I came back.

#

Back in the present, I have a creeping feeling I should address the elephant that isn't in the room with me, but in the changed streets outside. I'm tempted to leave the pub and look around again, check that reality really was fucking with me and I wasn't just hallucinating due to the lack of sufficient booze in my system. Another mouthful of warm bitter gives me the clarity of mind that I don't really need to leave a pub that shouldn't be here any more, just in order to confirm that things are different and not as they should be. While I look around the bar for any meaningful detail which might point to a solution or explanation, I slowly make a mental list of possible solutions to the weirdness, as they present themselves to my conscious in-tray:

First possibility; I've entered an alternate reality where the past thirty odd years haven't happened at all. I name that my 'Bobby Ewing in the shower' option, if you remember that season of Dallas? I don't, but I know it was an iconic TV moment. An explanation for my method of travel to this other timeline remains shrouded in mystery. Even for me and my flights of fancy, considering this scenario any further doesn't appeal. The idea doesn't hold water, and it doesn't even rank on the scale of probability that I'm starting to formulate. Not a waste though, following a Sherlock Holmes approach to deduction, you should rule out the impossible first.

Second version of events for me to contemplate; I could be part of a psychological experiment by aliens to see how I react, like a lab rat. Chosen because of my penchant for questioning the meaning of life. See above for likelihood. Also disturbing that probing has now entered my mind for a second time. You can go your whole life not considering being probed by aliens, and then it inexplicably occurs to you twice in an hour. Don't rule anything out.

Third thought; that this is part of God's mysterious plan? Not an explanation I can accept in the absence of any faith at all on my part, though if I'm wrong about that, I suppose whatever happened serves me right. And perhaps this is heaven after all? Peanuts and beer. That's a pleasing image. I like to think I have an open mind about all things, even religion, so I rank this option (marginally) higher on the probability scale than the anal probe.

Fourth; I'm now a time traveller who also changes clothes along with years, but I'm new to it so have some sort of time travel amnesia. It makes as much sense as anything else I've come up with, but I haven't had enough beer to overcome the rational objections and queries yet. I consign this thought to the unlikely pile, with a post-it note flagging the fact that the different clothes is also far stranger than I am giving it credit for.

Finally, as my eyes return to the bar area, maybe this is just a dream sequence in my life. This feels like I'm getting warmer but I can't get my head round how that would work in practice. In my admittedly limited experience, a dream sequence is quite unusual outside of bad movies.

Having found nothing of use in random conjecture, even though I'd let my imagination run totally free in the hope it would come up with something, I corral my wandering thoughts, and point them in a better direction, to put things together more chronologically. It had been starting to work before, when I'd been walking here.

So, rewinding to the last partial success in rediscovering my timeline, I know I'd drunk quite a lot in The Cali, and also in my flat before I'd left there for the evening. I'd been pissed off with everything in my life. This was my state of mind when I last had concrete memories that made sense. And just like that, my brain fires up a last-gasp attempt at putting the dots together and giving me an instant solution; is it as simple as the fact that, alcohol fuelled, tired, and fed up of the shitty evening, my body had decided what I needed was a little trip down memory lane, via the medium of either sleep or unconsciousness. And in the process of regular drunken sleep, or possibly through an alcoholic coma, I've ended up here, living in the memories of my past. I'd prefer the former dreamstate but will accept the latter as a prospect.

Taking another mouthful of bitter, I settle on this explanation of events as definitely being the most likely of all the options I've come up with so far. It is acceptable to my view of the world, is certainly possible, if not probable, and best of all, if it's true then this solution requires no action or particular further thought on my part. And as this is a dream, I can do whatever the fuck I want with total immunity. Ladies and gentlemen, we have a winner. I breathe in deeply, and the stale tobacco aroma welcomes me once more like an old friend.

I can almost feel the tightness draining out of the facial muscles, as accepting this dream scenario means a wonderful absence of responsibility, and also saves me going crazy trying to work out this strange experience. It's almost like happiness. As an added bonus, the fact I don't have the keys to get into my flat had been hovering at the back of my mind, and can now stop hovering and bothering me.

Following dream logic, it doesn't matter where I actually live, something will turn up to solve that little problem. I have beer and peanuts, and memory landmarks to look at, nothing else matters.

Now that it matters less and I'm not trying to force it, the realisation comes to me that if this is thirty odd years ago that it seems to be, I know where I should be living and it's not far away from here, just the other side of Parliament Street. I let my brain keep wandering in this direction, as a reward for coming up with an idea I like. There might be 'another me' living in my room, one who would be very surprised to discover an old man turning up, saying he was going to bed down for the night as it was his home too. I don't think that the me I'd been then would take this very well. The concept of being punched in the face by myself, intriguing as it is, doesn't rank high up the scale of attractive opportunities for me to pursue.

I pull on the brain reins. Enough procrastination and self-examination. If it's a very good dream, I'll find a bed for the night that doesn't involve sleep. If it turns out to be a bad one, then flying monkeys might eat me. In either event, the lack of house keys doesn't matter much. I wish I could stop obsessing about it as I'd just decided to, but my mind doesn't follow instructions very well.

I reach into my pocket to look at the time on my phone, putting my hand slowly back onto the table afterwards and staring innocently towards the bar so no-one notices my mistake. My reactions are automatic and don't countenance the fact that no-one would know what I was trying to do. I search around until I see a clock instead. A little before five p.m. I ponder my plans for the rest of the evening. My hand brushes against the chunky ashtray at the centre of my table, and if you were watching you'd just have seen my face light up like a child on Christmas morning. If this isn't reality, then cigarettes aren't bad for me any more. I don't mean they aren't bad in the generic health warning way, more in the bringing on death-related reaction way. I can smoke again. Without consequences. Hallelujah! Cigarettes are on that agenda. It doesn't matter how long you've given up for, there's always a part of you that longs for a cigarette and the comfort it brings. It might be illusory, but that's the hope.

"Hope..." From its vaguely helpful beginning, the voice I think I hear seems to have reduced itself to single words. My subconscious can remain sub if that's all the use its going to be to me.

I have the notion this current year must be sometime between 1985 and 1995 from what I've seen so far, so a little exploring might be in order. And some food, sometimes peanuts alone aren't enough. My mood brightens even more at the prospect of drinking in some of my old favourite pubs before they get changed or ruined. So, I now have a vague plan in place. Smoke. Down to town and see what happens to me there. Drink. Smoke. Back up to tour some of the pubs round here. See what happens next. Eat something. Smoke. Drink. If nothing dreamlike happens, drink some more until reality is sufficiently altered to make sense of everything else around, or makes me lose track of it completely. Then wake up. Hopefully not in the hospital.

I decide to walk through part of the University grounds first, to pay attention to the surroundings before it gets dark and to see whether my memory of locations was accurate. This is followed by a brief circuitous train of thought that if this is all created by my subconscious then it can't actually *be* inaccurate, but I argue against myself that my conscious memories of the past might be self-deception, and I'm altering the past to something more palatable. I get bored of that circular thought very quickly as there isn't any likely resolution to the question, and in all honesty, I don't care enough to try and find one. It was just a passing fancy as I left the pub.

I very quickly get bored of looking round the streets too. Most of them look the same as in the present day, or in recent memory, and the area around the Georgian Abercromby Square looks quite understandably much the same as it must have when Georgian was new. It starts to rain harder again, so I turn down towards Town and decide I'll be both productive and wasteful, heading into the dry warmth of the newsagents.

I pause as I'm just over the threshold, delighted at what I see. For some reason, this place seems so vivid, warm and real to me. I move slowly over to the newspapers themselves to do my productive bit, soaking up the smells and sounds of the place, as I pick up a paper at random to scan. This informs me that Prince Phillip hadn't forced Charles into marriage after all, according to the headline at least, but of more interest and relevance to me is the fact it is still the same date, October 17th, but it's now a Monday in 1994 rather than a Thursday in 2024. This fits, in a bizarre way. I would say that it makes sense, but clearly this would be an overstatement at best, and more accurately a lie. I get the sensation I'm being watched.

I glance around and see that this isn't my regular paranoia, and discover I am indeed being watched. I'd forgotten how much I loved this shop. I'm being stared at in the familiar 'you don't buy unless you read' way by the proprietor. I remember him so well. Ronnie Barker could have based his character in

Open All Hours on this shopkeeper, apart from the being funny element. I don't think I've ever seen the man smile. A twinge of regret comes over me that he's long dead now, and I never told him how much I liked him. Why would I? It would have been a very strange admission to make out of the blue, but I remember him fondly now. Or I do for about a second, until I realise that his narrowed eyes are still on the newspaper in my hand. I slowly place it back as though I'm holding a live grenade and step forward towards him.

"Twenty Camel Light... and a box of matches... please..."

I don't know why saying those words brings such joy but it really does. And his expression mellows from suspicious, to suspicious but eager to take my money before I change my mind. Open All Hours and the malfunctioning till come back to mind. A flash of panic that I only have those coins in my pocket abates and I grin so widely at the measly two pounds thirty he asks me for. His expression is a mixture of eager acceptance of money, and confusion at the grinning old lunatic in front of him. Jesus. I'm older than him, aren't I? That wipes the grin off my face and I leave, ripping the cellophane off and admiring the artwork on the packet, sniffing the unlit, perfumed tobacco hungrily, rediscovering how lovely that moment of opening a fresh packet of fags truly is. Some people love the smell of freshly laundered clothes I know, but for me, give me unlit tobacco any day of the week. I tap one out and look around, stepping around fresh puddles as I head to the corner, cig in my mouth like I used to. I want to eke every last moment of pleasure out of these seconds. It's been twelve years since my last cigarette, and I'm aware my current happiness and anticipation is about to be flattened when it tastes like shit, so that beautiful cancer stick can stay unlit a few seconds more.

I turn the corner, and there is the brick and concrete monstrosity of the Everyman Theatre. Fuck, but it's beautiful! The current version of the thing won awards I know but that version is just bricks and mortar to me. This is 'my' Everyman. I stand outside for a minute or two, just staring, and my eyes are almost tearing up. Fuck the walk to Town for a bit, a pint in the Everyman Bistro has to be done, for old time's sake. I take the cigarette from my lips to put it back in the packet before realising I don't have to. No smoking ban. The word "civilisation" acquires a new meaning. I move carefully down the steps, partly to savour the sensations and experience, but mainly as I have a dodgy left knee these days and I don't want to go arse over tit.

It's so much brighter than I remember, and surprisingly quite busy, though not too much to be able to find a comfortable space. I walk slowly down the aisle, glancing at the tables. No-one I recognise, or if I once did, I've long since forgotten them, and I wait my turn at the bar, looking at the pumps and wine lists chalked up before settling on a bog standard lager. Lager isn't really my drink these days but why not, live in the moment. I allow myself a brief moment of reflection, mainly centering on the fact while this is all very pleasant, it's been a fairly dull dream so far, everything considered. And I still have a nagging feeling that I should be remembering something important. I order, hefting the still very pleasantly jangly collection of coins remaining in my pocket.

Shelly. It has to be about Shelly. Wasn't this the time she said we'd first met? 1994? Not when we got together, but when we first met. I don't remember, but she'd told me once that we first met a couple of years before I thought that I'd hit on her for the first time. It must have been round about this year. To be honest, I don't remember much of what she'd told me about our first meeting exactly, I'd been distracted by her cleavage while she talked. It makes a kind of sense my dream would put me here if this had been our first meeting. I'd been talking to her yesterday, if it was yesterday, or back in reality. I'd gotten drunk and then gone to the pub after our phone call. I was still thinking about her then. Was this the plan my mind had? See and remember that first night, and somehow it would make things different? I snort loudly, ignoring the strange glances I get. Not fucking likely. But then again, if reliving our first meeting would get her out of my head it might be worth it.

I open the matchbox and strike one, staring into the flame. I have no idea why we got together in the first place. Aside from her tits, and there aren't a shortage of those in the World. Had I really loved her once? It was all a bit of a haze. I hold the match up and inhale my first cigarette in years. Take the beautiful smoke down deep. And almost cough my guts up.

#

Our marriage had lasted a little over two years in total. In a romance novel, the getting together would be a whirlwind (which I guess it was), the marriage would be tumultuous (I don't remember much of it), and the divorce sad, with breakup sex (it was angry and the sex wasn't with her). The only good thing to come out of it was Sarah. As least, I assume she's good. And mine. That's the cliché isn't it? The child that came out of the union was the good thing. The truth is, I haven't seen her or heard from her for nearly a decade now. A get well card after my heart attack, that was all. Sweet. It was more than I got from her mother at the time.

According to those who still knew us both, it had served me right, but a card wouldn't have been too much to ask I don't think. If I hadn't given her years of happiness, I'd at least given her years of my life. Two and a half of them. And a daughter. Probably. I don't know if the interpretation was a generic 'served me right' from our mutual friends, or a more specific reference to my girlfriend at the time, Shelly's 'replacement' as she apparently saw it, even though we were fifteen years past being together by then. And Kathryn (with a 'K'. I never got that right, it used to really piss her off) was young enough to be my daughter, allegedly. I think Shelly imagined our relationship as a hotbed of sordid sex and perversion which had been too much for my ancient and withered heart. Actually, the truth was that she wasn't even there when the heart attack happened, Kathryn with a 'K' I mean (I remember the 'K' vividly now for some reason). She didn't stick around for that long afterwards either. But before I start to weave a sympathetic picture, I should admit that my heart attack did actually happen during sex, just not with my girlfriend. And the sex wasn't very sordid, but it's true that it was probably far too energetic for me. And expensive. In both senses of the word. Still, the girl in question had waited around until the ambulance came. Who says whores don't care? Proper customer service, though not to a happy ending that time. If I remember right, she'd used the name Cathy. Or maybe that's what I asked her to do. It was a long time ago.

After the cancer scare in 2005, things had initially thawed a while with Shelly, who for some unknown reason had insisted on coming round and taking care of me. It was seven years after the divorce so we could be civil by then. I say "cancer scare", as that's how she referred to it for a while. I just called it cancer. Now she tended to call it a missed opportunity. Or "a fucking shame they caught it early enough". I accepted her being there for a while; let's face it, it was convenient and made things a hell of a lot easier, having someone to do things for me, but the positive side of the thawing didn't last long. It was more in the vein of an iceberg thawing than a defrost, and chunks started falling off quickly once it began. Once one of those fuckers starts to melt, it doesn't stop, and to keep the metaphor going, I felt like I was starting to drown. I could have eased myself away gently, but why would I? I just wanted out of the water.

I know that I had considered just stopping answering the phone, or not being in when she came round, but she might not have got the hint if I did that. And I'm not good at subtle, I'd just wanted her gone. As helpful as she was trying to be, I couldn't stand the woman's voice any longer. Her fake 'caring voice' was even worse than her regular voice, and that was bad enough. So I posted a note through her door instead. 'Thanks for helping. I'm fine now though. Can you drop the keys off through the letterbox? Thanks'. The second 'thanks' was added against my better judgement, to soften the blow and show my gratitude. She didn't see it that way, though. Even when I explained that I'd only added the 'thanks' for her sole benefit, and I didn't really mean it.

I'd let her screech at me for a few minutes, about how ungrateful I was, and what a bastard, which I could hardly deny though after the initial barrage, her rant had annoyed me quickly. After all, I hadn't asked for her help, had I? It didn't seem to help when I pointed that out either. I don't recall for certain if I was deliberately trying to antagonise her. It was possible, as the letter hadn't worked and she wasn't taking the hint and backing away gracefully, but I know that I'd suggested she wasn't doing a very good job of looking after me by shouting and screaming, and did she want to give me a heart attack too (how prescient of me)? I know I'd kept as much emotion as possible out of my voice, trying to sound level and logical, as that always bothered her. When she started hitting me, I think I was quite justified in the slap I gave her back. Not vindictive or intended to hurt, just enough to bring her to her senses. Okay, maybe a little more than just enough, but it didn't do her any harm. And it did finally shut her up. Briefly.

#

The way down to Town is a mixture of happy and depressing for me, and my inner whispering voice seems to have given up on helping me at all so I take in the sights. In some ways so little has changed. A flutter of happiness at the sight of the Magnet Bar and Hardman House Club, old stomping grounds, and a further flutter of delight at the lack of small supermarket chain shops, and even the presence of the one group of people I still remembered and recognised individually. The Big Issue sellers and other people begging on the street have been such a permanent fixture through the years that I know most of those faces by heart. Sadly, a number of them are still doing the same thing now, in the present day. I guess they must be good at it to survive that long. Reluctantly, as I don't usually do this, I give the first I come across, Peter I think, one of my precious pound coins. He grunts and turns to look for the next person coming down the hill. I try the same thing a second time with another face that rings a bell, though I didn't know this one's name, and this gets me a grudging, mumbled "thanks." Looking further up the road I know that I'll be out of pound coins before I reach the bottom of the street, so I avoid further eye contact. Shitty fucking dream. Could have at least given me a little gratitude for my selfless action. Or provided me more money in my pocket when I'd woken up. That was the depressing bit.

The street is little changed, alternate brands and less food outlets, more traffic, but the buildings themselves aren't very different. Sniffing, I light another of my cigarettes, enjoying the first drag a bit more this time, and head down towards the bottom end of the Town. I remember the pubs and clubs I used to frequent on Hanover and Paradise Streets but can't recall what should be further on down the main street, even before you get to the location of what is now the Liverpool One shopping area. This would be a major redevelopment in a decade or so, a multi-million pound shopping centre full of shops I wouldn't be interested in. And HMV.

"Shelly..." My monosyllabic subconscious is back, and this time the murmured word comes from the distance, prodding me to return to my previous thoughts and the slap.

The fight with Shelly had almost fizzled out. You might have expected fireworks or recriminations, but my slap had actually calmed her down. After a fashion. Something had changed in her eyes though. I remember I was puzzled by it at the time, but looking back on it now I think that might have been the end of the road for us, from her perspective. For me, she was already history, but I think somewhere deep within her she'd kept a torch flickering, thinking that one day we might rekindle whatever it was she thought we'd once had. She hadn't dated again that I knew of after the divorce, not seriously anyway, and she could even have been holding out for some sort of full-on reconciliation. The swipe of my hand through the air snuffed out any lingering flame for the last time, and strangely, actually made her more civil again. She'd enquired if I wanted anything else, and had said she'd be round the next week to see if I needed anything, even as she'd taken the key out of her purse with a grip so tight it couldn't mask what had been clearly trembling hands. She'd left it on the table and told me to take care of myself. Even kissed my cheek. It was extremely unsatisfying and not a little unnerving. I'd been wary, not knowing if this was a calm after the storm or I'd find glass in a casserole at some point in the future. But she'd kept her word and kept calling, completely civil and platonic, as though nothing had ever happened. As I recovered properly, it was her that had been the one to quite calmly inform me that she didn't need to call round any more, but was happy to meet up for a coffee if I ever wanted a chat. You can guess my answer to that. I'm assuming Sarah heard Shelly's version of events of what happened between us from her mother though, as I didn't hear from her at all after that, not even a Christmas card, until I almost died. Shelly stayed in touch though, filling me in on my daughter's progress and achievements over the years. They seemed distant and unconnected to me but I appreciated knowing, so we even met up once in a while. Until she'd bumped into me with Kathryn (with a K) for the first time.

Fuck, it was depressing here. I might not have been a fan of the shopping centre they built, with its bars and clothes shops and restaurants, but the place would still be a massive improvement on the miserable sight that meets me now. A multi-story car park and lots of other non multi-storey parking opportunities (if you liked leaving your car on waste ground and losing hubcaps). The Moat House hotel rises less than majestically over this vista, looking as depressed at where it lives as I feel. I thrust my hands deeper into my pockets, looking over towards the river and the newly refurbished Albert Dock. Neither holds much appeal.

That little itch at the back of my brain starts up again. It's easy to forget all this is wrong. If this is a dream as I've decided to believe, all well and good, but it still doesn't explain the details I can't yet remember from the rest of the evening in The Cali. I try to pull at those threads one more time, as it's a more productive thing to concentrate on than waste ground car parks. Most are loose threads that prove unconnected.

#

I stop at a place on the way back up the hill towards my home turf. The Egg Café is a bohemian (read sparse) place at the top of more stairs than I remember, off a side street. Musicians, artists, and students always hung out there so it had always been worth a visit for me if no-one was buying gear further up in the pubs nearer home. I know I'll be accepted easily now as part of the eclectic mixture of clientele. It was never my favourite place to eat, being far too vegetarian for my liking, but I need something in my rumbling belly and it's convenient and familiar. The door at the top nearly hits me as it swings outwards and the departing figure, a waft of flowing black coat and unruly hair, doesn't even pause to apologise or acknowledge me. Cunt. With a scowl I enter, taking in the crap local artists' watercolours that always hung on the walls and the candles on the tables, and I order a bowl of soup and some crusty bread. Reluctantly, I add a pot of tea to my order as I'd forgotten they have no license. I find a spot at an empty bare wooden table and wait. Something is broken apparently and they'll shout me when it's ready. I think that's what they say but I don't pay that much attention to the specifics. Instead I go for a piss to fill the time. And remember.

#

He hadn't followed to the toilets in The Cali thankfully, but the distant hope he'd be gone when I came back hadn't come to pass. Instead, the annoying little git had been staring wistfully back up at that fucking photo again, seemingly in awe of it. Fuck knows why, it wasn't very interesting.

"Do you know what Chaos Theory is?"

I'd sighed, clearly not likely to get any peace until I'd found a way to make him fuck off.

"Dropping water on the back of a tart's hand, and telling her the dinosaurs are going to eat us in the hope that you get a shag?"

He'd tilted his head quizzically. Clearly no sense of humour, or film quote knowledge.

"It's about unpredictability, how everything is intertwined, causality... just think of the series of events for poor Norma Jeane Mortenson. Happy, sad, tragic, if just one thing changed, one foster home, one kiss from DiMaggio, one casting decision for Niagara and the choice of peroxide. And there wouldn't have been a Marilyn... so many people wouldn't have been inspired by her... so many songs and pictures wouldn't have been created, and she wouldn't have been dead at 36..."

He'd seemed obsessed, and slightly creepy.

"So?"

He'd appeared disappointed at my reply.

"Never mind... so why did your ex's phone call rile you so much? Was it something particular she said?"

I'd grunted. "None of your business."

"You said she was being nice again?"

"Did I?"

Yes, he'd been right. That was right, she had been nice, hadn't she? Suspiciously nice. That 'calm voice' she faked. And asked questions about me, and what was going on with me. That was her icebreaker. I remember now. Some of it anyway. I hadn't wanted to react to him at the time though, so I'd chugged the Jameson chaser and gone back to the bar for more. I hadn't asked him if he wanted anything. The chair had scraped and I'd grabbed the back, admitting to myself that I was a little more drunk than I thought. My eyes had locked onto his eyes, where he seemed to be deliberately avoiding my gaze. Why had I talked to him about Shelly at all? And what had I said?

I chuckle to myself now as I shake and zip up, I remember having had that specific thought. I'd let it sweep over me and away at the time as it didn't really matter and I'd been more focused on getting more alcohol in me, but part of my subconscious obviously remembered. Why had I confided in this stranger, and what had I confided? It wasn't like me. I don't do that. Maybe I should seek him out when I wake up. If I really can't manage to remember what Shelly had said to me, then maybe I'd told him and he'd recall what had happened. Though that would mean talking to the twat again. There was something about his manner I hadn't enjoyed.

When I'd returned from the bar he'd continued as though I hadn't been away, sipping his own beer that barely seemed to have gone down.

"Would you have done anything different? Back when you were together, I mean? Could you have saved the marriage?"

I'd ignored him. It wasn't my fucking fault. And there wasn't anything to save. And it was none of his fucking business. And I didn't want to think about her.

"Anything could have made a difference. You've heard of the Butterfly Effect?"

I look up now, the uttering tickling at my mind, almost reminding me of something I'd heard more recently. The tickling sensation passes before it finds the answer.

"It's a good movie. Great ending. Cunt kills himself."

He'd tilted his head to one side like a parrot.

"They pass each other on the street and don't recognise one another? No-one dies. Is your only reference point what happens in movies?"

"Director's cut... Cunt kills himself. Much better. And no, I do music and literature too. If there was no Marilyn... there'd be no Candle in the Wind, fucking result! Butterfly Effect..." I'd wobbled my head ever so slightly like I was retrieving data from an old computer bank. "...Sound of Thunder by Ray Bradbury, excellent story, though we're back to dinosaurs again..."

He'd ignored my rather funny and clever comment as I'd laughed at it to myself.

"Don't you ever think about it though? Being able to change things for the better. One choice, one decision and everything gets better for you, Jack. It's a fascinating thought isn't it."

I'd coughed a chuckle, still pleased with my earlier comeback.

"Is this where you tell me I'm at a crossroads? Make me an offer? I'm too old to play guitar and I have no soul, so no good for music and Faustian pacts... ...sweet Helen make me immoral with a kiss..."

"You mean 'immortal'?"

"I know what I mean..."

"I don't think you're quite in that position... 'You have   picked   me   out. Through a distant shot of a building burning'."

I'd grunted, or maybe snorted. It was clearly a quote, but I'd had no idea what of, and wasn't going to ask the fucker and give him the pleasure of telling me. Though I'd known I would probably try and google it later, as not knowing quotes drives me nuts. If I managed to remember what he'd actually said. Something about a building on fire.

"No, your references are for fame and fortune, and I think we both know that isn't on the cards for you, Jack. There is one parallel with those luminaries in terms of limits to what can come to pass..."

"And what's that then? Eternal salvation, as I think you need something called 'faith' for that, and you're on a loser if you're recruiting for the God squad. And what can come to pass... more self-inflicted poor health and pass from the borderline to full blown alcoholism? Redemption? Why bother? I'd too old for that shit... Yippee Ki Yay motherfucker..."

I hated that he'd managed to get me talking, and talking so much. I prefer my conversations short and to the point these days. And wasn't quite sure how I'd got onto a Die Hard quote. I think I'd lost track of what he was saying somewhere.

"No." He'd taken a long, slow drink of his pint. "Nothing quite so abstract or... well, nothing like those things. I mean you share things in common with Marilyn and Robert Johnson... the difference a single moment in time can make, and their possible lives if something happened differently. You share that with them. We all do but especially you I think Jack. Ripples. Limits. Whether or not you believe in a higher power you have to believe in consequences? You live them every day, and they're just the ones you can see or track. There are so many we never see and never imagine. As I mentioned, the Butterfly Effect can apply to everything. What do you think your future holds, Jack?"

I'd waited for the pearl of wisdom or the offer of a copy of The Watchtower. The corners of his mouth had crinkled slightly in amusement.

"You have sixteen hours left to live, Jack. Quite probably less..."

And then he'd fucking grinned at me, as though this would be a good thing for me to hear.

It hadn't been exactly what I'd been expecting.

His pronouncement had hung in the air for near on a minute as I'd digested, opened my mouth to reply, and then closed it again. I couldn't think of a witty comeback, of anything come to think of it, but I'd swallowed hard as for some reason I believed that he was telling the truth. I'd forced some words out, trying to laugh it off.

"So... you're a fortune-teller? You're going to tell me how to avoid that?"

I remember at that moment my mouth felt incredibly dry. He'd shaken his head sadly.

"No... and no... I can't think of a thing."

And suddenly, he'd laughed, loud and long, his eyes flicking from me to Marilyn and back. It had broken me out of my shock. I'd stood up, slipped a little and grabbed the chair for support, reaching out with my other hand to grab the collar of his jacket.

"What's so funny? What's so fucking funny?"

He'd laughed harder and easily dislodged by fingers from his clothing as I'd slumped back into my seat.

#

I don't know how long I sit in the café, losing track of time as I go back over what I remember of that conversation again and again, searching for clues or hints in what I'd said or what he'd said. The mention of a butterfly though. I know now why the voice I've been hearing in my head is so familiar, it's his. He's obviously affected me more than I realised. The large chunks of bread and the pots of tea have soaked up a lot of the beer, leaving me in serious danger of sobriety before too long, so I choose to head further back up the hill towards where I'd started.

I wander aimlessly for far too long, ignoring my surroundings in the hope that something further will return to my recollections, and I'll remember what else he might have said after that last comment and the laughter, and it might explain what had happened more clearly, and why I'm still imagining his voice. For all the good it does me. Anything beyond that point stays teasingly just out of reach. I try another bar on the way up but it's loud and bright and doesn't suit my sombre mood, so I only stay there 'till I've finished one drink.

The pub known as Bonaparte's hadn't existed for long as I recall, only a few short years in the nineties, but I had some very good times there. It was at the end of an innocuous terrace, on a corner, and was a strange little bar catering for the artsy crowd, wannabe bohemians, and people looking for somewhere with extended hours after regular closing time. I push the door open, eager for alcohol and more familiarity, and order a large glass of Cabernet Sauvignon, choosing a table by the window, facing towards the back wall bar. Again, there's such a wonderful feeling of comfort and warmth about being somewhere I like. Not too overlit, candles in wine bottles on the tables, half filled with drinkers, the sounds of Portishead's first album piping through the music system. I like it very much. The place is like it should be.

We used to come here after kicking out. It was always a good mix, and there were usually a few students who we could sell weed to. We only ever spent an hour or so before moving on, but I get the strangest sensation that this is the right place for me to be. A place of very fond memories, which is unusual for me. It's the negative things in my life that force their way to the forefront of my brain usually; those times I can identify with a bad thing, or pinpoint why something had gone wrong. There's a certainty about those moments, and they're the go-to fixed points in my past that never leave me.

This whole bizarre evening has been pleasant enough so far, but I'm still hoping for something of note to happen, some epiphany or big event, and I'd worked out in the previous café that if I stick to places which I know well, the odds will be better that I'll see someone I used to know eventually, and maybe even see 'myself'. That would make my being here less random. I have a pang of regret, almost a physical pain at one connected realisation. My friends are still around in this time, unlike now.

Brian is dead in the present, cancer. Twelves has gone, no-one quite knew how, but he'd vanished twenty years ago, presumed dead. Benny, Mike, Emma; all gone or lost touch. I can't think of anyone else left alive who I'd known during this time. It comes as a bit of a shock to me to realise that Shelly is quite literally the only one left from those days, and I haven't even met her in this timeline yet. Unless I was going to see her tonight. Maybe that was what this was all for? Remind me of once being attracted to her? That crazy little thing called love? Random thoughts keep whirling around, but they mostly end by returning to thoughts of Brian. This is the second time I'd found myself thinking about him since I woke up in the cemetery. I force the memory of him away again. It's too difficult.

I have a moment's regret that I never joined the social media revolution. Maybe I could still find old friends and catch up that way if I tried, maybe I should. Reconnect? This could be the prompt I need, and why I'm dreaming all this. To find people again. It's ironic I suppose. After my first aborted attempt at a career fixing computers, and having realised that I had the knack for it, I'd tried again after we got married; a career I mean. Software this time. Windows 95 had just come out, and the web had been new and fresh and exciting, and already a new way to access porn. I'd taught myself quickly and for some reason it had come easily to me. It had been the perfect time to get started, and before I knew it, I'd been pulling in a decent amount of money by making and fixing websites, with a minimum of effort needed on my part. The early social media private messaging and bulletin boards sound dull, but I was really into them for a while. As the years passed, I'd become bored with it all, and by the time the modern social media boom took off I simply couldn't be arsed. I'm sure I could pick it up again pretty quickly if I wanted to though, even track down the names I remembered. It was an option.

I pause, then dismiss the option with a little regret. The people I knew in the nineties are about as likely as me to bother using social media now. Once the novelty had worn off it was all cats, conspiracy theorists, vegans and right wing wankers. And what would happen if I did actually find someone who remembered the old me. "Hi, want to talk about dead people, failed dreams and how the world used to be so much simpler and better?" Depressing conversations and lies. Not something worth my aspirational hopes. And would we even know each other any more? Like one another? The ones I think I'd like to see are either dead or presumed dead, and the others... acquaintances or friendships based on being off our heads together. Some of them I don't think I'd ever talked to when I was sober or straight.

The only drug I take these days is Warfarin, and I don't even bother with that half the time. Perversely, I light another cigarette and drag deeply on it. This year I'm in must be around about the time that I stopped dealing, so this might be my final glory months, my last grasp at decadence. In fact it must be very near the end of my carefree and careless days. I'd stopped taking anything much illegal by the time I was dating Shelly, and was certainly clean before we got married, only a couple of years from now. Stopped except for the occasional joint that is, but that doesn't really count. I suppose I was still young enough to do whatever I pleased back then, and the derangement of the senses was a wonderful thing with no thoughts of consequences, apart from feeling like shit the next morning, until I took something to sand the edge off. My intake of substances might explain why I don't remember meeting Shelly for the first time. I don't actually know why I gave all that up. They were good times for me. Did I think I was growing up, settling down? Did I do it for her? I don't recall. Was I a martyr or a saviour for giving up everything bar alcohol? She certainly didn't take anything to excess, a smoke now and then but that was about it. Was I trying to fit in? To do the right thing? I pick a chunk of bread out from my teeth with my tongue, annoyed with myself that I'm thinking about her again.

Life was simpler in some ways back in the eighties and nineties. We knew what we were doing and whether it was right or wrong we just chose to do, or not to do things, and lived contentedly with the consequences. Today, it's more virtue signalling over virtue. I'm not a virtuous man, I never have been, but I like to think I'm honest. Judge me on my actions, not on what I say. I think that lesson came from my grandmother. I miss her. Even now, in this dreamtime of the nineties she'll be long dead. But I think she set me up to be a good man? I'm an arrogant cock I know, but not a bad one. I don't think so anyway.

My peripheral vision catches something at the bar, and it takes a moment for my brain to fully catch up and switch away from self-examination. Two girls, jeans and leather jackets with make-up and expressions that tell me they're students, re-inventing, are talking to a young guy in a sweater with round glasses at the corner of the bar, clearly trying his luck. Without too much success it seems. They're obviously enjoying the attention, but unless the drinking goes on for a long time he doesn't have a shot. There was something that had bothered me when I'd first noticed them though. The right hand girl, longer hair, couldn't see her face, chatting to another boy in a check shirt at the other end of the bar. The one with the shorter, curly hair turns to talk to her. Pretty, glasses, three earrings and a nose stud.

But the sweater boy is watching too closely, it had been odd, and now, stepping forward to block the view of half the bar, he tips something into the glass of wine with a shaking hand. I'll be honest, I don't know exactly what it is, but it can't be anything good. For years, decades, there were warnings of leaving your drink unattended, date rape drugs, but I've never actually heard of it happening in real life or to anyone I'd met. The guy barely looks eighteen, and not exactly poor by his clothes, and bland. He doesn't look the sort.

I'm halfway back to the bar before I even realise that I've moved, and I don't remember deciding to do anything of the sort. I think some half-baked idea may have occurred subconsciously, about something like that not happening in one of 'my' pubs, in a place I remember fondly, and which I'd viewed as 'mine' when it had been one of my dealing haunts. But that hadn't been a plan or even a fully formed thought. Before the girl can even turn back, I walk past as though heading to the toilet and extend my elbow, aiming for and hitting the wine glass perfectly, knocking it over and making it fall to the floor, which hadn't been the intention but works just fine, smashing it and splashing red wine at the legs of those around. They jump almost as one. The nose stud girl is the first to look down and confirm it was her drink, like claiming this might bring it back. I stagger a little, as though drunk, while she calls me a wanker and then pulls herself up short, seeing my age, an advantage of maturity it seems, and reigns in her anger as I apologise and insist on buying her another. She checks her jeans for red wine stains and tells me it's fine but I've already attracted the barman, who is ready with a cloth. I'm obviously old so non-threatening, and don't appear to be too completely hammered so I get served with a replacement for her. The two girls and check-shirt move off to a table away from me, comforting the one who had tragically lost half a glass of wine and got a full one to replace it, and make sure that each of the others is okay after such a traumatic moment, throwing an annoyed backward stare or two at me.

Sweater boy hasn't moved, but his face is coloured with a blush and I turn in his direction now, away from the bar. I'm sixty, and as I said, appear non-threatening. But I've grown up here, and I know how to turn that on its head. I lick my lips and feel my eyes narrow slightly, my face pinch tighter, as I appear to lean casually towards him and thicken my accent.

"If you try anything like that in here again, I'll break your fucking skull son... you understand me?"

It's muscle memory. My eyes expand wider, not blinking and lock onto his. There is just the hint of a dangerous smile on my lips. His face flushes, whether through embarrassment at knowing he's been caught or fear I don't know, probably a little of both. Student as well I suppose. I don't think he even notices that he gives me a tiny nod that he understands, but before he can respond with any more than that, I turn and head for the toilets, quite pleased with myself and the order of events. And for still being able to intimidate a little student prick.

I pause to look in the mirror after pissing. I don't look at myself very often, but the word grizzled wouldn't be inappropriate. Nose that had been visibly broken in the past, bags under the bloodshot eyes, stubble, creases (not yet wrinkles) showing a weathered face. Yes, if a face like that had threatened me, I'd have thought twice, old as it looked. I don't know why I thought I was non-threatening. I tentatively try a hangdog expression and see it reflected back, just a sad old man. Useful to know. I pull my facial muscles tighter again to return to the nasty bastard I'd quite liked. And a nice thick accent to a non-local always adds that edge too. I allow myself a little smirk again and see it doesn't suit my face. You can tell it's meant to be a smile, just about, but it could equally be a nasty sneer. Fuck, I feel old looking at him in the mirror. When did I get so old? And my hair, not yet gray but certainly not black any more, hence the harsh short cut. I shrug. Fuck it.

I head back to the bar to reward myself with another wine, and as I put my hand in my pocket, feel the outline of paper in the small jeans pocket. Pushing my thumb in I find a folded note. A wonderful, old fashioned paper five pound note with a picture of George Stephenson on it. Large wine then...

Back in the main bar, just as I sit down, I catch a glimpse of two figures heading into the back room. A leather jacket and a red hoodie. And I know instantly. Me and Bri. I'm here, and he's here. Alive. The old us. I gulp the wine. We're here. I'm here. Brian is here. Actually here. This was what I'd hoped for. Everything else fades into the background. I hadn't known it myself, but the wave of mixed pleasure and nausea confirms this was what I'd been hoping for the most. Fuck, I want to follow them. I want to follow so bad. I pull out another cigarette with a slightly shaking hand and light it. Only two things stopped me moving already.

One, the back room we've just entered is a 'Pool room', one room, one single door in and out, and other me has just got the key from the barman to use it. So there's no way of casually walking past or observing. If I went into the room I'd be told to fuck off and have to make my excuses as, reason two, what the fuck could I say? "Hi Jackson, I'm you. And Brian, great to see you again, you've been dead for years, shall we get fucked up?" And they'd stare at this sixty year old sad excuse for a man, thicken their accents, put on the face, and tell me again, a little more dangerously, to fuck off. There was nothing I could try to intimidate them. They'd laugh in my face.

Or worse. He'd look at me and might actually recognise what I was, and I'd see his thoughts on my own younger face. What the fuck happened to me to turn me into that, is this what I become? It might be my own subconscious making this up, but I don't think I could take seeing that reflected in my own eyes. I glance up at the shadow hovering over my table. A guy in his thirties maybe, green shirt and black trousers, smart but not posh, casual.

"Mind if I join you for a moment?"

I turn my attention back to the door at the rear of the room.

"I'm not bent. Fuck off."

I don't bother trying to be intimidating this time, he's just an unimportant annoyance. He laughs.

"Me neither..." He pulls out a chair and sits himself down without invitation. "I just wanted to say, saw what you did with the dickhead at the bar. I wasn't sure what you were doing at first but I was sat by the door, heard what you said. Something in her drink?"

I nod absently, still thinking about the back room and how to get in there without being seen.

"Can I get you a drink? Just to say thanks? I know the girl, sort of... and you paid for hers too, didn't you?"

"What? Yes... okay... whisky... thanks..."

Doesn't do to turn down a drink and as was becoming apparent, I don't know anyone here, not to talk to. None of the faces at the tables rings a bell, not even the barman. And talking to myself isn't doing me any favours. The distraction and free drink might be good for me in my current state. He nods approval and disappears off to get served, coming back with two large Jack Daniels'. I haven't drunk that brand since... well, since about the nineties I realise as he holds his glass up to toast. I suppose I have to say something.

"So... you know her?"

He inclines his head. 'Long-hair' is chewing the face off 'check-shirt' and 'nose ring almost-victim' is smoking a cigarette and staring out of the window. I offer the guy who bought the drinks a smoke but he declines, which is good as I'm getting through them fairly fast. As his polite refusal gives me an extra smoke for later, I carry on talking to reward him.

"Friend or fuckmeat?"

A twitch on his face tells me he doesn't appreciate that term, and it's probably unrequited love, but he's in no place to call me on it as I've just saved her arse. Probably not her actual arse, though you never know.

"She's a friend... well, friend's sister, but I appreciate it all the same."

I make a non-committal acknowledgement of the fact.

"So who was the bell-end? A regular here?"

He shrugs.

"Don't think so. You're not then?"

I smile to myself.

"Not for a long while."

"Can't be that long, this place only opened a few months back."

Fair cop.

"Not been back round here for a long while, heard someone mention it serves late so thought I'd try it... is the Planet still open? Planet X?"

I used to deal in that club sometimes, and it was dark and dirty, but just big enough to get a proper look at myself and Brian without being obvious. If it was still operating, then there was a good chance that's where the young me would be heading after here. He holds his hand out and I shake it as there isn't really an excuse I can think of not to.

"Paul..."

I grudgingly tell him mine.

"Jack..."

I wasn't going to tell him anything, as, well, why the fuck would I, but I wanted information.

"No, it closed a year or two back, I think. You don't look the type... I mean most of the people in there were... no offence mate..."

I shrug.

"None taken."

I assumed he only knew the club by reputation, as age wouldn't be a bar to being a regular so much as attitude. And I could always namecheck Doreen, the owner, I knew enough about her to blag the fact we'd met before. But if it was closed down then it probably meant young me would head to The Casa instead. I nodded towards the back of the bar.

"What's... in the back room? Saw someone going in before..."

He glanced over his shoulder.

"Pool room. Currently dealer's room I think, if weed's your thing? You'd be okay if you've got the money. They're not that picky"

I didn't know it had been such common knowledge, assumed our trade here had been just word of mouth from friends but I was quite pleased. And amazed I used to be so stupid as to let all and sundry know what I was up to. Amazing I'd never got arrested actually. It wasn't like I sold once or twice, it had been my main income.

"Alright, are they?"

He raises his hands to signify he either doesn't know or care greatly.

"Black one's alright, other one doesn't say much and he's not as friendly, bit of an unpredictable fucker."

I should have been offended but if anything, it makes me happy. I nod sagely.

"Predictable is overrated."

#

We talked for a bit, and my decades of foreknowledge came into play as an early Oasis track came on and I proved very informed about the band to his surprise; here was a scruffy old codger who kept up with the new music. Trying not to get caught out, I'd shown off a bit and ended up talking about The Doors for some reason. I don't know how much time passed before I realised it was approaching closing time bell, and if I hadn't already missed other me leaving, then he would be very shortly. I drank up, telling Paul I was going to head to The Casa for one if he wanted to join me. It didn't hurt having someone to talk to, and he seemed interesting and impressed enough with me that he wouldn't be too much of a pain. I wanted to see what younger me was doing, and he'd be a useful cover. As he'd missed the unrequited love nose ring girl leaving he agreed, and we'd got up and wandered off towards the next place.

One of the things I always used to love about Liverpool when I was growing up was the clubs that didn't seem as if they would be clubs from the outside. I think it goes back to the jazz clubs, and further to the dance clubs of the war. The Casablanca was one of these. Up three steps at the end of a row of terraced houses, a bulb above the front door the only thing to mark it out, but to all intents and purposes just someone's house. Inside were two bars, a dancefloor, a cellar seated area and a wonderfully eclectic mix of people from every walk of life. A lot of people from my neck of the woods and further into L8, students some nights, the Liverpool artsy scene and Everyman crew. Actors, dealers, old men in trilby's, no affectation (apart from the paintings of the film the place got its name from). It had been bought by the dockers later and nowadays was a bright and far too clean bar which had killed any appeal it held for me. But back then. Back 'now'. Well, I loved it.

We knocked, paid our entry, and headed in. The evening had picked up in the last hour or two. Booze had flowed nicely, I'd somehow fallen into a conversation with someone not too objectionable, and everything was so familiar that I'd almost forgotten that none of it was real. None of it. In reality I was probably passed out on a pavement somewhere in my own vomit, smiling in my dreams as I pissed myself. We bought two beers and headed downstairs, stopping at the bottom of the stairs for a tray of chips each and heading to an empty booth. It was like an American diner in the cellar. And as we sat eating and drinking, in silence this time, I looked over Paul's shoulder to see a familiar back of my own head two booths over, and that as clear as a well-lit cellar, there was Brian, facing me. That was what hit me like a double punch. The wave of relief and fondness sweeping over me at the sight of his grinning face, deep in conversation with 'other me'. And the knowledge he was dead. And that meant this evening couldn't be real.

I don't know when the last time was that I'd seen him alive. He'd never told anyone he was even ill, and by that time, according to his eulogy, it was already too late. We'd seen less of each other once I was married, like all good cliches, but had still stayed in touch, and been on a number of benders. He'd never judged any of my choices. And dead just before he turned 35. I can't help looking for any indications of illness now, though fuck knows what they'd be. He has less than six years left from this point. I almost didn't go to the funeral, couldn't bear it. I had to be drunk enough that I could get through it so it's all a bit of a blur, but I had to be there. I owed him that much.

I look over at his face, creased with life and laughter, so vibrant. Just like it should be. It would be a filthy joke he was telling at the minute. The man knew the most perverse jokes there were, and the more inappropriate the better. If you'd picked a dozen people off the streets and put them together as potential friends, Brian and me would be the last pairing you'd make. He was always so upbeat, always smiling, never still for a moment. I was always a miserable fucker, my own sense of humour so dry and my temper so hot you could use me to defrost a fridge. That had been an observation of his. But from when we were kids, we'd just clicked, and for years we were never far apart from each other. If one decided to try something, the other had followed without question; if one had a problem then the other would try to solve it any way he could. I don't think we ever thanked each other for anything, didn't need to. Once we even dated twins. His fucking hated me. After a couple of weeks, so did mine. Brian dumped the girl he liked so much, just like that. Women weren't hard to find when you were young and strong and had cash. Friends were harder. And lasted.

"Yes, now you remember him, how long has it been again since you thought about him?" That's the whispering in my ear little shit with his high pitched voice again. It's been a while since I've heard him. He never needs a reply, always rhetorical. This isn't a memory of our actual conversation though, it's as though he's still talking to me again now.

I hadn't realised I was staring so much until Paul asks me what's wrong. "Nothing" I say, and carry on eating, but keep watching from the corner of my eye, entranced. Brian doesn't look exactly like the man I picture in my mind, memory is a tricky beast. He isn't as clean cut as I thought he'd been, or as clean shaved. Plus he looks rough, like he's been up for more than just one day; that wasn't unusual for us. But it's definitely him. Unmistakably him. I even recognise the blim burns around the neck of his t-shirt, from careless nights and cheap resin. A thousand things race through my head at once, the foremost among them 'how can I save him?'

I've had a decent life, a 'good innings' as they say about old people, but Bri wouldn't have a chance at a long life, and that isn't fair. What force had picked me rather than him to survive? And why couldn't he have had the extra years I had until they found it? No, scratch that, why hadn't they found it sooner? I laugh at myself silently as the thought of telling him the future comes to mind. "Hey Brian, you don't remember me, but I'm the same guy sat opposite you right now, looking thirty years younger, but as I've come back in time, I just thought I'd tell you that you have cancer, you might want to get that checked out, if they catch it early enough you might not die like I remember?" I can't even remember what flavour he had right now. Whether it's one of the lucky ones they might have had a chance of helping with chemicals or a knife. Couldn't hurt though could it? Telling him. Well, apart from the punch in the face I was likely to get.

Living Brian caught me looking at him and whispered something to other me. They both laugh, and I look away. Hearing my own laugh isn't pleasant.

"... and she just walked off..."

I look up and nod, pretending I heard what Paul has been saying but it turns out that's the end of his story anyway. I let my gaze sweep over the rest of the room, wondering if there were any other people I know in here. I used to know a lot of regulars. I have this vague inkling of an idea, that while I can't say anything to Brian myself, I might be able to find a way of talking to him through an intermediary. One side of my brain is working out who I could claim I was, a relation or friend of someone not here, plausible but not too obvious. No-one sparks any recognition in the room though. A few are vaguely familiar but no-one I'd have known well enough to be able to casually bring up the subject of cancer. I sink into my pint and try to pay attention to Paul, hoping that something will inspire me.

"...married?"

I guess that was aimed at me so nod, phrasing my reply carefully just in case he's talking about something else.

"Didn't work out for me..."

A flash of anger at her again.

"Never marry an ugly woman... they might look hot on the outside but inside they can be ugly. Find that out beforehand."

I'm paraphrasing something funny I'd once heard. Paraphrasing it into something not funny it seems.

"Kids?"

"Not really, I was in my thirties..." I let my mouth answer while my brain does other things, scouring every corner for an idea of how I can warn my friend. "... she was mid-twenties but never seemed like a kid either. More grown up than me I think."

A grudging admission. One I don't mean to make.

"...I meant do you have kids?"

"Oh... one..."

I should feel something, talking about Sarah, but no. She existed. Exists. Is alive. Or Shelly would have said something.

"I've not got any. But plenty of time..."

Plenty of time. That brings back another conversation from earlier in the evening with a jolt. What the fuck was that 'sixteen hours to live' all about? Was that the length my dream will be? Have

93

I got sixteen hours to save Brian? I grin, reminded of a Flash Gordon movie quote, and Paul must think it's at his comment. The thought of warning myself, younger me, rather than Brian, hadn't even seriously occurred to me yet. I have a sneaking suspicion that the me of a few yards away wouldn't be anything like I remember myself being at that age. Centre of attention, popular, funny. That was how I'd thought of myself I know. One thing I'm fairly certain of is that he'd have no time for an old man wanting to chat. Buy something or fuck off, no interest otherwise. Not unless there was something in it for younger me.

"Upstairs?"

I agree without speaking and follow Paul. There's no point in staying down there. Too bright, no plan, nothing to see.

We wander into the back room, where the music ranges from obscure northern soul to student-friendly indie rock, and more proper sixties and seventies actual rock. It's as I remember, dark and dank and you can keep to the wall and just watch. Paul finally seems happy to shut up and soak in the ambience too, so we scan the room and half empty dancefloor. As it's a Monday the place isn't full, but given the other lack of options for after-hours drinking around here it's never really empty either.

My eyes land on a curvy blonde dancing badly but provocatively with two guys in denim. I think I fucked her once. It proves a pleasant distraction, watching her arse for a few minutes, and I'm on the verge of bragging about having had her when I realise it would sound like a very unconvincing lie, given my current age and appearance. Not impossible from what I recall, she wasn't picky, but I decide not to mention it anyway. More people are arriving and I think a number of them are acquaintances I used to know. No Twelves or Benny, but some faces from my old neighbourhood. It's a melancholy recognition. One face stands out. He was always a regular here in the club, but was one of the most pissed off looking men I'd ever met, even more than the shopkeeper from the newsagent's earlier. Unlike the shopkeep, this one wasn't actually angry or even unfriendly, just built the way so his natural demeanour was that of a bulldog licking piss off a nettle. I forget his name but I'd liked him too. Jesus, he may even still be alive somewhere, scowling and looking slightly less fed up the more stoned he got. I get the urge to say hello but resist. The more I drink the more I want to talk to people. I just don't want to have to listen to what they might decide to say back.

It's hard to know how to strike up a conversation, even with the warm glow of whisky, beer and bad wine swilling around my stomach and fogging my natural reticence to socialise. The other me hasn't emerged from the basement yet, which is a surprise as I would only have been in the club to deal, and that was always more difficult in the brightly lit cellar. I should have been against a wall in a dark corner, much like older me is now. Paul had wandered off somewhere a while ago, which had left me free to crowdsurf with my eyes and think, uninterrupted. I was beginning to seriously suspect the man in the pub with his dire predictions is a part of this dream too, and I am in actuality genuinely slumped in my flat, a now-empty bottle of whisky beside me on the floor.

It was getting busier by the minute, and the dancefloor was almost full. I keep thinking I see flashes of my old familiar black leather jacket, or the brightness of Brian's hoodie through the crowd but it never proves to be the case. That, and several times I'm drawn back to watching the profile of a girl with shoulder length dark hair and a slightly out of proportion nose. Each time, I momentarily wonder if it's my wife. Not my wife right now, at this time we hadn't met, and in the present she's very much ex, but I think of her as being my wife while I watch the form of that girl. There's still the possibility this is the night we'd first meet, even though I have no recollection of that.

I'd brought Shelly here a few times later on in our relationship, and she'd loved the place almost as much as I did, though for different reasons. She loved to dance, and seemed to have no inhibitions here. She was built for this type of nightclub dancing I think. Not the formal ballet or ballroom stuff, just shaking it on a dancefloor, not caring who watched her or what they thought. Her jeans too tight over her full ass, her top cut too low to dance like that without attracting attention. But she hadn't cared. I never danced with her here. Not because I couldn't dance (I was no great shakes, but I could move when the mood took me), it was more that I had an image to uphold. Even though I'd stopped dealing by the time I brought her to the Casa, there still the vestiges of wanting to be viewed a certain way by the acquaintances I had. I thought the aloof, acerbic front was what made me liked. Or respected at least. I was a bit of a dumb cunt back then.

Shelly saw straight through me of course. She never said anything, but she didn't need to. I didn't need to try and impress her because I knew that I couldn't. She just accepted what I was. And no matter how sharp the barb or tone, nothing I said or did fazed her in the early days. It took years of practice for that. Don't get me wrong, she didn't judge me or challenge how I was, just... wasn't bothered by it, and maybe that was the appeal for both of us. When I used to watch her dance here, in this back room, I didn't even used to get jealous of the attention she received. It wasn't that sort of place. There were plenty of guys and women cruising to pick someone up, but her freedom on the dancefloor, I wouldn't call them dance moves so much as throwing herself into the music, tossing her head and hair, those thin lips smiling like she didn't have a care in the world, they were mesmerising. Shaking her tits and ass as much as her feet or arms matched the rhythm, a lot of people looked but I knew she was quite capable of dealing with any unwanted attention, and with a smile. She wouldn't have thanked me for intervening. I would just be happy to watch, knowing I'd be in her later.

Maybe I'm being sentimental, or maybe I'm just pissed enough, but I can half remember why I was with her tonight. You could always see the lights reflected in her eyes, even from across the dancefloor.

I'm shoved out of my reverie by literally being shoved as a scuffle breaks out beside me and I move deeper into the back room, away from the problem as bodies converge to throw out the troublemaker, whoever he is. There's no sign of Paul so he might have gone by now. I raise my wrist to check the time, forgetting I don't have a watch and I'm drunk enough to find that funny. I haven't worn a watch for years. This time and place is rubbing off on me. And then, a flash of red from across the room, through the jostling bodies. I blink to try and clear my vision as much as possible from the smoke.

It isn't just that I've located my other selves. That shitty little four eyed wannabe rapist from Bonaparte's is talking to them. He seems to be buying something from other me, I recognise the way my hand passes his to slip something into his fist. I don't know what it was but I didn't sell shit like that, I know I didn't. I was certainly selling him something though. As he slinks away, Brian and younger me share a laugh and a punch on the shoulder at a joke. Taking the piss out of the lad, I hoped, for selling some dried oregano or tealeaves. That at least would be something.

I see him move around the dancefloor and towards a group of girls dancing by themselves in the corner, off the main area. I don't know why I move again but there's something about his smug little face that makes me want to wrap my hands around his skinny throat. So I do.

#

It was cold outside. I hadn't objected to being manhandled out. Well, technically I had, but it didn't do me any good so let's pretend I hadn't. I did object to the fact the little cunt had stayed and actually been looked after by the people around, asking if he was okay. I'd caught a glimpse of the leather jacket as I was shoved towards the door, and had hoped it meant that other me was going to do something to help, but why would he?

I pull my jacket tighter and watched my breath in the night, or early morning air. There are three fags left in the packet so I light one and turn in a small circle, the night or early morning spinning not unpleasantly, not quite sure what I should do next. I'd been expecting some sort of revelation or incident but to be honest it's been a pretty dull evening apart from getting thrown out, and even that had been an anti-climax. They'd been surprisingly gentle, if firm, in guiding me outside, even making sure I didn't fall down the steps before slamming the door shut. On account of my age, no doubt. I check my pockets. £6.30 left. I could wander round until I wake up, head back to my old flat and see if something happens there or... there were always one or two places that didn't bother with last orders at all, and no-one much cared. I could afford a couple more drinks yet. I have a mental image of the Nigerian Club on Parliament Street, dilapidated, old fashioned dancefloor, metal grille over the bar. Blood on the dancefloor, like the song. That seems apt. I'll try there, see if it's open and if my face fits tonight.

"Hurry up Jack, but make sure you take your time, and pay attention..." The light voice whispers to me on the wind. By now I don't care if I'm imagining things, pissed, or I'm if still being guided by the somewhat hypocritical little bastard. It's difficult to take my time to hurry up, or vice versa, but I accept the challenge.

I start weaving along Hope Street, paying a little more attention this time to the changes to buildings. I'm drunk enough for it to be interesting to look. It isn't really that different than it appears in the present day, though one word could be added to any descriptions of what I see now. Tatty. The gentrification of the area was only just starting and let's just say that lots of the buildings look a little the worse for wear. The new buildings I was familiar with from the twenty-first century aren't here of course, the restaurants and posher bits, but the side streets don't seem to have changed at all. That's nice. I like the backstreets of Liverpool. Unlike many other figurative backstreets a lot of these actually are 'back streets', even in name. Back St Bride St, Back Percy Street, Back Bedford Street. There's something fitting and quite unpretentious about them. Knowing that their place isn't in the limelight, but unapologetically proud of what they are. Refusing to accept their identity is anything less than unique and remarkable, much like our city.

I glance down the right hand streets at the Unity Theatre and Ye Cracke pub, liking the fact they are still the same as always but I stop myself by the brick walls surrounding the Blackburne House Arts Centre. The suitcase sculptures on the pavement haven't been created yet, and Mount Street, rising from the City Centre, is still linked up to Hope Street. It was such a critical area that had seen so much over the years I knew, the poet Adrian Henri lived (and would still be living as I stand and look!) only a few doors down. Fat fucker might even be in, looking out of the window at me. I wave just in case, not caring that it would make me look ridiculous, and in the absence of knowing which house, I wave the greeting down the middle of the road for a moment or two.

Opposite me, the corner of the building where people used to congregate. All the Beatles history around attending the Institute and Art College here, it all looks just the same as it would have in their time. Forget all about Penny Lane, Strawberry Fields, Mendips on Menlove Avenue, anywhere mentioned in the songs or on the Beatle tours that would already be running. Aside from Hamburg this place is probably one of the most important spots in the creation of Liverpool as a creative force on the sixties. It wasn't just Henri, the other two famous Mersey poets, Patten and McGough had lived at the end of the road, Lennon and Sutcliffe had rented, or squatted, in a flat a few dozen yards away on Gambia Terrace, and Ye Cracke would see all the creatives there, musicians, artists and painters, poets, playwrights, just scant years before they all changed popular culture. Might be why McCartney picked here as the location of his Fame school I surmise, deciding that's an insightful intuition on my part, rather than being fucking obvious.

I know I sound like a fanboy, I'm really not. To be honest early Beatles music isn't that much different from the other Merseybeats at the time. Their mid-career hit stuff is okay but there's better by plenty of others in the mid-sixties, who might be less prolific but far more innovative, and the late stuff is just up its own arse. I'm genuinely not a big fan. Some cracking tunes here and there I'll grant you, but it's ones like *Rain* and *I Want You* rather than the best known tracks that are worth a listen. Or do I still like to be obtuse for effect? I choose to ignore my own question, and take my time rambling like the wind told me to. I might find a hint or signpost in the thoughts that catch my attention.

McCartney did some great stuff afterwards, and Harrison some really great stuff (even if bits of songs were nicked), so I think I'm willing and able to judge things on their own merits. Of the poets, Henri was a great painter, McGough a poser, but I'll admit Patten was very good. I'm pleasantly drunk and digressive now I know, but why the fuck not? I think this is a special place and fuck anyone who doesn't agree with me. I wish I'd lived in a place with so much going on like this had in the fifties and early sixties. I'd have made something of myself. We had Eric's and Probe Records but... well, I never went to those places and you get the feeling that they were a lot less fun anyway. I deserved to have had a chance with a place like sixties Liverpool. I definitely could have made something of myself. Every other fucker did.

I carry on up the street, my mood a fraction more sour. The sixties were probably nothing like that in reality, but that was what the books said it was like. And books never lie. Not the ones you believe.

I halt at the next corner, the Lost Boys garden and St James' cemetery opposite me over the road. I toy with the idea of going back down there. I'd woken up in the place, so maybe I was meant to go back there to wake up again? That would be nice and self-contained. Wake up there as something is due to happen to me in a few hours, according to the twat in the hat, though I've forgotten what it is. I'd better be well rested and back home just in case. I don't know why I still can't quite place what it was that was due to happen, but I'm sure there's something. Something important. The wind seems to sigh.

I set off again, on past the railings, ignoring the prostitute on the other corner. This is a big area for whores and junkies, I know that from back in the day. Don't get me wrong, there was a lot of smack and coke about everywhere, but we all functioned fine on that. Well, in the main we had, was just how things were. But these streets were where the proper committed junkies and whores congregated, before they got moved on to another neighbourhood. I turn left, planning to cut through Back Percy Street and through knocking-shop central to the Nigerian club on Parliament Street. I sadly don't have enough money left to take advantage of any of the other admittedly skanky hookers I know will be around this time, as cheap as I also know they are.

I turn the corner, seeing a whore I think I recognise as one I've fucked more than once when a ringing starts in my head. I stumble forward, and regain my feet just in time for the sensation of just being hit over the back of the head by something very solid to register. Just before something hits me in the face, and the World goes black.

THREE – 17th October 2024

I blink at the brightness. And wince at the pain in the back of my head, reaching up to my face to check for damage, still in a half daze. My nose seems intact but my fingers have blood on them. The figure opposite lifts his lip in a half sneer.

"Bad night?"

'Confusion' isn't really a big enough word. My mouth opens and closes silently, and I see the half pint of bitter on the table in front of me. My mouth is horrendously dry and worse, I'm even more horrifically sober once more. A wave of nausea comes over me and I reach for the drink, draining it in five fast gulps. I blink again, several times, quite deliberately, to clear the slight watering. It's an odd habit I've picked up somewhere through the years, and when I do that it must look like I'm having a seizure.

"You shouldn't drink, it's bad for you..."

He lifts his whisky and knocks it back in one, getting up and heading to the bar. Nothing makes the slightest sense.

I reach up to my nose again and wipe away another smear of blood, licking my finger absently as I try to put my brain back together. I need to piss, badly, and that takes precedence so I scramble to my feet and head to the toilets, along the corridor and to the right, only half aware that I'm back in The Caledonia and my dream is over at last. Or my nightmare, I'm not sure which it really was, but at least I'm back in a reality where I belong.

I empty my bladder then move to the sink, looking into the mirror above. There's blood under my nostril but nothing broken that I can see. I reach for the back of my head and regret it, as I touch where the pain is and find a sizeable lump. I run the cold water and splash it on my face several times, clearing my vision and sweaty skin, and look at my reflection again before drying, in case I've missed any. I have a large two inch scar on my left temple, above my eyebrow, but not a fresh one. Years or decades old by its appearance. My fingertips slide over the rough skin as I try to remember how I got that.

I shake my head once more, dry my face, and move my eyes back to the mirror. I'm very confused, just when everything should be making sense again, dream over. I should be in my bed, or on my floor, or in a hospital bed. The fact I can't remember getting that scar is just an extra piece of the puzzle. It definitely seems the kind of thing I should remember, but everything is in such a haze I can't be sure if this is just a temporary blip. I'm not going to strain my brain trying to remember such a small detail at the moment. There are more immediate issues. Like how did I come to be back here?

I doubt very much that I'd have fallen asleep over my pint. Not that it would be the first time alcohol and tiredness had taken it upon themselves to find me slumped over an unfinished drink, but I don't think I'd been quite that hammered this time. And if it is really the same night as the one I'd left for my dream, which I sense that it is, then I couldn't have been asleep for very long. They were still serving, and it had been well into the evening when I'd first arrived. But the weird little man in the peaked hat had gone by the time I'd just opened my eyes again. That was one positive thing, but it meant a decent period of time must had been and gone, as a ten minute nap didn't seem enough to have discouraged him from staying put to be a pain in my arse for even longer. I instinctively check my pockets but my wallet and phone are still there, so he hadn't knocked me out and robbed me. Having just been without wallet or phone for several hours, it's nice to discover a fact that proves I'm definitely back in the present and have all my own things again. I mentally walk through the few moments before I'd headed into the toilets. There had been someone in that same chair opposite me when I'd opened my eyes, someone who looked like they'd been in the chair a while, and had acted like he knew me. Well enough to be a cheeky young cunt anyway. But he was nothing like the drinking companion I'd last seen in that seat. This man was in his twenties, dark, unkempt hair, leather coat. I couldn't remember any more than that from the brief moments I'd seen him. On balance I decide the best thing for me to do is to drink more. It may not be logical, but it's one of the few ideas I have for what to do, and it's always a good fallback option, whatever the situation. If you drink enough you don't care so much if life makes sense. Whatever happens to me, I'll never lose that mantra.

I look to the left as I come out of the corridor from the toilets, and mutter "bitch" at the new photograph of Marilyn still hanging there taunting me, and that makes me feel a little better. The existence of the picture tonight is something tangible, a change I can blame anything on is very welcome, it gives me agency. If anything, she looks even more depressed than she had earlier in the evening. It was obviously a posed photograph, so why would she or the photographer choose that look? It didn't matter enough to warrant further consideration though, and it's a perverse consolation to me that she looks so pissed off.

He was already sat back at the table looking out of the window as I walked back, a fresh pint of beer and a whisky in front of him, and a matching set in front of my chair. I'm not going to look any gifthorses askew, so I sit and lift the glass, taking a large swallow without acknowledging him. If he wants anything from me, he'll have to ask. A free drink gets you nothing. He keeps looking out of the window, oblivious.

He was what you might call pretty. Not in a gay way. Symmetrical. Unkempt in a manner that fitted his face, and didn't detract. But just a kid. As I think that, he turns his head to look at me and those eyes... They stare right through me as though he knows what I was thinking. Those are eyes that have seen shit. I say something then, just to stop him looking.

"What happened to the twat who was here before? The smiling one?"

He shrugs carelessly, whether meaning my question is unimportant, whether he didn't know or just didn't care not clear from the movement.

"How did I get this scar?"

I point at my head. Then actually fucking blush, feel the heat rise in my cheeks. I don't think I've blushed for years but I have no idea why the hell I'm asking such ridiculous questions he couldn't possible know the answers to. I can't stop once I've started though.

"Have I always had it?"

He just stares, not even bothering to shrug this time. It's unusual to be able to convey disdain without moving or changing expression but he manages to do just that.

"I could tell you why your nose is bleeding if you wanted to know that?"

I take another mouthful of wonderful beer and bob my head to indicate I'd appreciate that. Any fragment of knowledge would be welcome.

"How?"

"I hit you."

I feel my eyebrows go up of their own accord. This seems to be a day for unexpected answers. And for my face making its own decisions. It doesn't even occur to me to ask why he would have hit me, and I feel strangely calm, when his statement should, at the very least, make me angry or curious. Like I say, I'm desperate for any facts or certainty at all, and something that explains an unknown, like the blood on my nose, is doubly welcome. I can't work out how I'm back here.

"Could I ask you... another question..."

It has been formulating in my mind for a while now, minutes and even hours, and getting that last response made me certain if anyone can answer it, he can. I still didn't know why I assume that. He knocks back his whisky, as though he's been waiting for me to ask, and nods permission.

"What the fuck is going on?"

The question seems to sum everything up quite nicely. Encompasses and encapsulates most of my many questions quite succinctly, I think.

He laughs. A quite high laugh. And his eyes lock on mine without an answer.

"I can't remember... I talked to my ex-wife earlier tonight... everything beyond that is... fucked up... and even that... I can't remember what she said... it pissed me off but I don't know why... I don't even know why she called me..."

I'm almost pleading for a grain of re-assurance that he knows something that can help me put my life back together, if only a few hours of it.

"Are you sure she did? Does she even have your number?"

"Of course she does, she..."

I'm stopped in my own conversational tracks. No. I'd changed my mobile and I don't have a landline. And I deliberately hadn't told anyone the new number.

"She... I... she called me... I know she did. I remember..."

I wasn't going to let go of the one single thread that links me to my reality. That unexplained detail can fuck right off for now. I don't know how Shelly got my number but she did, and she'd definitely called me. It was the one fact I've been holding on to throughout, and I'm certain of it. A little crinkle on his lips makes me think that he's fucking with me. Rather than getting angry, another level of strange calm sweeps over me, it might be resignation. If the one dependable anchor I have is being questioned, is there any point trying to fight the rest of it?

"Are you trying to confuse me... because you really don't need to... I've had a weird dream, I can't remember several hours from earlier this evening, and I have no idea who you are. Or where I've been. I'm fairly sure I haven't gone insane, but I'm not totally ruling it out. Are you even real?"

"Want me to punch you in the face again? I could do that for you, help you answer that particular question?"

I shake my head, the lump on the back of it giving a little throb to remind me that it's still there.

"Can you tell me anything? At all?"

The guy tilts his head slightly, considering, biting his lower lip in thought for what seems like an age. I drink to fill in the seconds.

"You pretty much fucked up your chance..."

Unhelpful.

"Thanks, but enigmatic doesn't work in a paranoid delusion... do you mean that I fucked up my life?"

His head tilts from side to side as he picks the most unhelpful words for his answer.

"Well, I think we both know that's true Jack, but nothing you could do about that right now. Your life is what it is. About tonight I meant. Where you just were... didn't try very hard, did you?"

I wish I was able to smoke. As if by telepathy, he pulls out a packet of Marlboro Light and inclines his head to the main door of the pub in invitation. I get up, understanding the nod and leading the way. He follows, and no-one else in the pub even acknowledges us. Outside it's cold, and my jacket offers little protection. He offers me a cigarette, lighting two with a Zippo and holding one out to me. I take it. I haven't smoked for either a dozen years or twenty minutes, right now it doesn't seem to matter either way. I drag deeply, taking the acrid smoke down easily and gratefully.

"It was a dream? I was supposed to realise something? Remember something, Do something?"

He leaves the cigarette drooping from his lip as he looks up and down the road.

"Was it? Are you awake now? Or still dreaming? Did you think of that?"

"It fucking feels like I'm awake. The back of my head hurts like a bastard."

As I mention the lump I automatically reach back to touch it, and wish I hadn't. The pulse of pain does make me wonder at his question though, the answer to which might explain the current weirdness, as well as what just happened in my own past. Is this whole evening a dream, including right now? Had I never made it to the Cali at all? Am I actually back in my flat, passed out drunk on the floor in my own drool and piss, ghost of Christmas past and Christmas present and all that. Like a Muppet Christmas Carol. It is a light at the end of a very dark, long and fucked up tunnel. I get a sense of déjà vu. Has this explanation occurred to me before?

"Only fucking with you. You're very much awake Jack. You should get out of the habit of thinking about your life in terms of films and stories though. Life isn't like that. It doesn't make sense."

I just accept he knew I'd thought about a film and it doesn't seem at all strange.

"What are you...? Are you supposed to be some sort of angel? A Clarence bringing me to a wonderful life?"

He sneers without trying to.

"Do I look like a fucking angel? And what did I just say about films? You just don't fucking listen, do you?"

He takes a deep drag and exhales more smoke than he seemed to have taken in.

"... or remember even the most basic things. It isn't a wonderful life for you. You'll be dead in less than nine hours remember? You were told that quite clearly..."

The prediction roars back into my consciousness. My response comes out far more pleading than I intended or expected.

"Sixteen... he said sixteen..."

"You've just wasted seven of them..."

I can feel the tension in my body as I take my turn to inhale the smoke as deeply as I can. I've held it together remarkably well so far I think, but I'm reaching the limits of my tenuous grip on sanity.

"Why? Why me? Why this, why do you care what happens to me?"

The sharpness of his eyes fastens onto mine and he looks through me once more, causing a shiver in the nape of my neck.

"A lot of questions. Let's see... I don't know... I don't know... don't know... and I don't care..."

I grasp my own right wrist with my left hand as subtly as I can, aware my smoking hand is starting to shake and not wanting him to see.

"Please... just... give me something... I don't... understand... any of this..."

He smiles at me, seemingly pleased at my increasing agitation.

"That butterfly effect shit from earlier... it's a fancy name but it's true... about everything... the smallest thing can impact in so many ways on so many things... but the story you mentioned earlier tonight, the Bradbury one... what's the main point of that, the moral?"

His tone has changed. This seems like a lecture, a lesson. My natural inclination would have been to take the piss but I'm on the edge, and this might give me some fragment of sense to work with, so I play along, taking a deep breath and searching my memory for the answer to his question.

"I haven't actually read it but... from what I know from the film... actions have unintended consequences... going on a time travel safari hunt and killing a single butterfly in the Cretaceous could mean over time there's a change in natural selection... it could have been key to the gene pool... without it reproducing, over millennia it could change life and create monsters so the moral is... well, every choice you make can have consequences you could never foresee or predict."

I can talk like that when I want to, and I was quite proud of myself for both remembering the plot, and delivering it in what I thought was quite an eloquent way. Like I said earlier, I haven't always been a total waster 24/7, I've held my own in conversations with intelligent people in all walks of life. I met a lot during my working life. I held down a job very successfully for years. Still have one, technically.

"Bollocks!"

He shakes his head and throws his cigarette to the floor, stubbing it out with his boot and heading back inside. As a drip of rain hits my face I sigh and do the same, with the feeling of being a helpless puppy. I followed like that helpless puppy, but deep inside I feel like the puppy has just had a kicking, and had been put in a sack ready to be burned alive. He was at the table waiting for me to sit, still in teacher mode.

"You really shouldn't rely on films... they take liberties, change things... don't reflect reality or what they come from... you should really read the story. It might help you... you'll have to be quick though. You know, being about to die and all..."

Some laughter sounds like shards of glass. This did. Our glasses were full again though he can't have had time to go to the bar before I followed him back inside.

"One, it wasn't about an intentional action or choice... something happened, something you might not even notice or think important, but the ripples from that one thing can spread like... well... ripples... and there's no telling what they'll impact and eventually change. It isn't a linear outcome like you describe... the alterations may be imperceptible, everything in existence is so interconnected you might never be able to see or work out what links a cause and an effect... and intended or unintended doesn't come into it... so no point in overthinking."

The words all come out totally without emotion, quite matter of fact, like he is no longer a person, just a vessel for this litany of spurious anti-existentialism. The cunt.

"And of course it's a book, a work of fiction. There's no such thing as time travel is there? This isn't literal. You can't jump in a time machine and change things by choice. Life doesn't work like that."

"So..." I try to piece together how any of this shit is relevant to me. "There's something I should have done or said in my dream... which would have made some sort of difference somewhere, to someone... which would have somehow... though I won't be able to see or work out how because I'm so fucking thick and because life doesn't work like that... I should have done something that will mystically save my life and make your sixteen... or nine, whatever, hours, go away? Can't you just make me dream it again, and tell me what to do and I'll do it this time?"

"You really are fucking thick, aren't you..."

He puts extra emphasis on the second word, extending it to four times its normal length, and pushes a beermat forward to the centre of the table.

"Rule one, no do-overs... if you'd ever bothered to read that story of yours then you'd know that too... second, I haven't the faintest idea what you could have done when you went back, though I'm guessing whatever you did spend your time doing wasn't helpful. Because you're back here, wasting my minutes. Too focussed on your younger self I imagine. Hubris? Do you really think your own past is the only important thing that's ever happened? And as to saving your life, how many times do I have to tell you. You... will... be... dead... in... nine... hours... or... less. That isn't a negotiation Jack, isn't an option, I'm telling you a straight fact. I thought you liked those?"

It wasn't a threat, it was a tired purgation of the inescapable. He added another fact.

"You will have a second, fatal heart attack... nothing can prevent it..."

A glint of satisfaction is in his eyes though, and emotion, almost gleeful, warms his tone as he continues.

"Do you know Xeno's arrow paradox?"

I stare at him, waiting for an elaboration, the detail he just revealed not registering yet. I get exasperation, pity, and derision in the same look back.

"Of course you don't, it isn't in a film. Never mind. Xeno was just a plagiarising bastard that liked fucking with people and trying to make people think in a different way. I doubt you have the faculty to understand what he said anyway, but just forget about trying to change history. Thinking like that won't help you. That nugget is for free. Wherever or whenever you are, in the moment... that's all that matters, those seconds and moments you're experiencing real time. Just pay attention to them. Try actually listening. It might be a novel new experience for you."

He looks expectantly at me, like a single word he just said helped me in any way, or explained a thing. A few seconds after he told me about my death, my comprehension caught up with my hearing and I may have zoned out. When he told me I was going to have another heart attack, I heard little of the following words, the dawning fear pushing its way forward to demand all my attention. Even my fucked-up mind knows this was something I have to concentrate on. Another heart attack. A fatal one. It was too specific to be inconsequential chatter, though he'd dropped it in quite matter of factly. I might be in the middle of a fantasy, or a nightmare, but when he said it, I believed him totally. I have form after all, been to that rodeo before, if not to the fatal part. I regretted the taste of fresh ash in my lungs. I wasn't sure whether his offer of a smoke had been benign or to try and help me on my way. I'd nearly died the last time. And it scared me. Not the dying, the pain. That word doesn't even come close. The agony. The being ripped from the inside. It scares the shit out of me.

"Did you know your estranged daughter is on her way to visit you... Sarah isn't it? She'll be the one to find your body tomorrow... and as she won't get the chance to tell you, and as I like to bring joy wherever I can... congratulations, you're going to be a grandfather."

The words enter through my ears but their meaning doesn't sink in. Or I don't comprehend it. I'm still locked onto the first bombshell. Very gradually, the additional information permeates everything and brings my full and close attention back to the continuing, rambling and casual conversation he was having with me, one which I wasn't even a part of. It was just him talking. He hadn't even paused for breath and wasn't even bothering to look at me, his gaze wandering lazily around the pub as he kept talking.

"...poor kid. Well I suppose I should have more accurately said that you're *currently* on track to be a grandfather.... The shock of finding your body... yup, that's not going to go well. At all. She won't be thinking about your corpse for a while afterwards. She will eventually of course, though not with much in the way of fondness, it's going to be your fault

123

after all. Bet you never thought of yourself becoming a murderer, not even a unique one who kills from beyond the grave."

His head slowly turns and his piercing eyes fix back onto mine, timed to perfection.

"... and losing all of her family so close together... you don't need any of the butterfly effect philosophy to guess which way that's going to push her, do you?"

The lump on the back of my head pulses as I struggle to digest the hammer of predictions I've just received. I say nothing, slamming the whisky down my throat and looking at the empty glass, waiting for it to refill of its own accord. It doesn't, and his eyes never leave me. He mouths three words very deliberately. The shape of his mouth is underlined with sick amusement.

"A... serial... killer..."

He actually chuckles, then holds up a hand to stop the words I haven't found to speak.

"No... seriously, before you bother to ask... I told you, you can't stop it... I can't stop it... no, there's absolutely fuck all you can do to try and change that... and why do you care anyway Jack? It's not like you do anything with your life... or care about hers if we're being brutally honest, and I do think very brutal honesty is often the best policy. I told you before, not everything is about you anyway."

He follows that with a smile of such fake sweetness I'm relieved diabetes isn't on my list of ailments. That actually occurs to me. There's only so far you can be pushed before nothing has any meaning, and things literally can't get any worse. My brain was trying to find a joke or distraction so I didn't have to deal, and I think he knows that, but he doesn't show any signs of stopping. From a recalcitrant and reluctant drinking partner, he's warmed into a flow which he's clearly enjoying. I interrupt with words I hadn't meant to say out loud. I wanted to say something to stop him from telling me anything else about my future, but I hadn't meant to say this particularly. It seems something within me needed to respond to his accusations and justify myself. And maybe it was another attempt to stop further revelations.

"I tried... I thought about... I wanted to change things for Brian..."

I blurt it out. Partly to shut him up, but partly because it was true. Yes, partly so I didn't have to think about the things he'd just said about my daughter, but partly with an unbidden spark that there might still be a hope of saving my friend after all. I have a nagging guilt that I haven't thought about him for so long before tonight, and I have no idea why that is. If there's even a remote chance I can help him... He'd been almost a brother to me from when I was a child. Family in all but blood. When had I stopped remembering Brian? I could pretend it was a conscious choice because memories were too painful but that wouldn't be true. To be.... brutally honest... at some point in the past, I don't know when, sometime after the funeral, I'd stopped thinking about him completely. I can't say it was to get on with my life. That would at least have been a reason. If this was the reason for the... insanity, I'd make up for it willingly. I was happy to.

"I could change things. Warn him..."

His steady gaze studies my face. Just long enough for the glimmer of hope to start and grow within me. So he has a larger target to aim to crush.

"No you couldn't. Brian's dead. A thousand years ago..."

The bastard pauses for effect again. Then plunges back into his talking which is now as irritating as the smiling little fat bastard who had started all this.

"Technically the last millennium so I can say that... where was I... yes, there's nothing you can do to change the now... the upcoming death... you could try and call an ambulance I suppose, pre-empt things, but they'd find nothing wrong with you... nothing new anyway... and spinning some story about fate and knowing your future, or lack of it... with the amount of alcohol in your bloodstream, they'll just write it off and... here's the real bitch...

another of the facts you love so much... from this point on tonight, whatever you do or try to do, you'll still end up back at home... it doesn't matter what you might try, you *will* still find yourself back on the floor of your flat, clutching your chest and gasping for air. You're a dead man walking... well... sitting..."

The fear and tension that had been physically building in every fibre of my body since the first mention of a heart attack, unnoticed by me, makes my hand start to shake again. I push it under the lip of the table so he won't see. I totally believe him and I need answers. Why? Who was he? What? I manage to ask as succinctly as I can.

"How... what are you?"

He gives the first genuinely happy smile I've seen on his lips, pleased to be consulted on the matter.

"I'm just a man... with a message... nothing profound... nothing mystical... and I'm not here to help, I really don't care at all about you, your wife, your child, your life... in a few hours you won't even be a distant memory to me. I'm nothing special. Though I do enjoy my job..."

He drains his glass and reminds me quite casually that it's my round, as though this is a regular conversation about nothing of any import. I find myself getting up and going to the bar to order.

How long has it been since I've seen Sarah now? What was the last thing I said to her? It creeps up on me as I wait to be served. This was the subject he'd obviously wanted to see me think about and I can't help myself. I try to remember loving her, but that emotion either never existed at all or is long since vanished. I don't hate her, or even dislike her, I just don't know her. She was born eight months after I married her mother, two after I realised that shouldn't have happened. She was born when I was deep in a conflicted madness of not being able to do anything about my situation, so I hadn't left straight away. Even I'm not that much of a bastard. You can't leave someone on the edge of birthing because you don't love them and made a mistake knocking them up. You either do it earlier, or you stay a year or so, be decent about it. I know she's my child, on paper at least, but she's always been a mother's girl. Later always sided with her mother. I don't blame her for that. Bitterly, I realise I don't even care about Sarah enough to blame her. The alleged fact she is carrying a child surprised me, I'd never thought about being a grandfather. It simply hadn't occurred before. The implication my dead body will kill my grandchild cuts me a bit though. And 'losing all her family'. What about Shelly, where is she in this?

I pull out my mobile to call, trying to remember my ex-wife's number. I haven't called it for years, it's always her phoning me, but one good thing comes out of her phoning me earlier this evening, that her number is in my 'recent calls' list. Half expecting something to stop me from doing it, I find the number and hit connect, indicating to the girl behind the bar with my free hand that the whiskies should be large ones at the same time, my conscious brain doing one thing and my body at the bar on autopilot. The other end rings. And rings. And rings.

I give myself a mental shake as the same noise continues. Why am I believing any of this? Yes, it's been a batshit crazy evening, and nothing has made sense up to this moment, but neither does what I've just been told. It's all too much to take in. I try to take deep breaths, every few rings of my phone, again and again like a breathing exercise I'd once learned for dealing with physical pain. I don't know how long I stand here like that, rhythmically exhaling, but I eventually have to stop as my drinks are on the bar, the girl waiting for my money, and the ringing sound grating, grating, grating. I pay and shut off my phone as there is clearly going to be no answer. The breathing exercise itself hasn't done any good, but it had given me something to concentrate on for half a minute. My mind comes back to the point of exploration it had left, minutes before. What might Sarah look like now? It's been so long, but she must be older than Shelly was, the first time I'd met her. Everyone said Sarah had taken after her mother, physically. So must look similar. I close my eyes and try to picture the face she might have now.

Shoulder length black hair, green eyes, slightly aquiline nose, distractingly thin lips, neither short nor tall, ample breasts, ass verging on the edge of fat, but not in an unpleasant way. I think that was what Shelly had been like at the same age, that's the picture I have of her, so I imagine our daughter might be similar. With a sour look under the skin of her resting face, ready to emerge with a sneer fully formed in the near future. The inner bitch emerging with age. And my grandchild. What would that look like?

Would? It won't look like anything. It will look like a dead baby, and would never grow to look like anything else. I feel nauseous. I'm not squeamish but I don't want to linger on that image. There's no benefit in it. And no point.

I hadn't realised my eyes had closed. I open them and carefully gather the four drinks in my hands, at the same time forcing myself to concentrate on something less painful and uncomfortable. It isn't difficult. I'm happy to forget the unwanted impressions. Was there actually anything he'd said which had been backed up by solid evidence of anything? This... this man... is a physical person, and doesn't seem to be giving me any spiritual guidance or hope. I have a lump on my head I can't explain, a blackout period, and a lot of bullshit. And I haven't questioned the fact he admitted that he's recently punched me , something I have no recollection of. Why am I taking any of this on trust alone?

I return to my earlier premise. If Bonaparte's and the Casa were in a dream, then who is to say this isn't a dream too, the same dream. The only reason I'd discarded that theory was the fact this man, who I don't know, had explicitly told me that I'm not currently dreaming. But what is more likely; that two preternaturally well-informed total strangers, who seemingly hold me in contempt, and who I've inexplicably listened to rather than telling to fuck off, have predicted the timing of my imminent and unavoidable death and the death of my family, and enjoyed my pain. Or that I've simply hit my head on the coffee table when I fell over after drinking at home, and this is still the ensuing drunken and weird dream. My own subconscious revelling in sticking it to me while it remains temporarily in control. The pain in my head emerging might mean I'm close to coming round or waking up on my floor. The mystery scar is a subconscious hint I've hit my head on something as I fell.

Yes, this is by far the most probable explanation. I lick my lips and imagine the tension ebbing out of my shoulders as I tighten my grip on the drinks, careful not to spill any. There is nothing to prove that a single thing this imaginary man says is true, and the most likely explanation is very clearly that I'm dead drunk somewhere and will wake up soon. Maybe in this mysterious nine hours. At that time, my dream self will die and I'll wake up for real. It was just a shame I couldn't have stayed in the nineties. That had been an enjoyable experience. I'd enjoyed it there, I realise now. With the added bonus of seeing my friend again, if only in a dream.

I construct every angle of this new version of reality quickly, and I like it very much. It makes sense. Jumps in location, time, narrative, knowing things you can't possibly know, thinking about things long forgotten. Had the phone call from earlier been about our daughter, was that what had upset me and got me so drunk I'd passed out on my floor and landed here? That would explain why she'd suddenly appeared in our conversation out of nowhere. Was it guilt? Yes, I'm liking this explanation more and more by the moment. I can rationalise. Were the men talking to me here just aspects of my psyche, reminding me of what I used to be? The way they acted towards me, condescension, disdain, amusement at the state of me, wanting to maximise my pain. I don't like to admit that this could be how my subconscious views my current existence, but I can't deny it's a distinct possibility.

I put the drinks down silently, not wanting to look at him or break from what is working out nicely for me now, and I leave for another piss, old man's curse. I didn't remember the scar because it wasn't there in real life. The scar was... representative of something, like dream things are... could be my fall, but could also be something else. I was supposed to pay attention to something, wasn't I? I have nine hours, like in Mission Impossible. I wash my hands, smooth my hair back with the water, splash some on my face. The two men are almost familiar too, aren't they? The man from earlier, the grinning dick in the hat with the Marilyn obsession... had I seen him once before, years ago, at a protest somewhere? And the guy outside in the long coat... hadn't I noticed someone like that on my one overseas trip, a hedonistic week in New York. Shared a smoke with him at the Chelsea Hotel, a painter I think? Or sculptor. Roadie? I'd dragged up their faces again for this.

I'm much calmer when I come back through into the bar area. Even the fucking photograph on the wall annoys me less when I view it as though it's just a physical manifestation of something or other that annoys me. I sit down easily and raise my pint, about to challenge this reality out loud and tell the man to stick his ideas up his bony arse, and to get the fuck out of my continuing dream.

"You're deluded Jack. Deluded, and totally fucked."

Roadie shakes his head sadly. He isn't going to play along, that's clear. He isn't ready to give up control, and this is his reality after all, not mine. I drink my pint and so does he. He can say what the fuck he wants, as a figment of my imagination, but I've decided I'm not going to argue with myself any longer. So of course I do just that.

"So... let's say all this..." I stretch my hand out theatrically "is actually true... and I'm about to..." I can't believe I actually make air quotes, without irony "...die... so what's all this butterfly effect shit about? Never mind... I'm assuming you're not here to gloat... not just to gloat anyway... So what do I need to do next, Mr Miyagi?"

The fixed smile on his face brings back that nasty shiver of unease, real or not. I remember now why I believed whatever he said. His eyes bore into me, pushing at my recently constructed justification for everything. It collapses in on itself, under the weight of just his eyes.

"Don't know, don't care... but do you really think I don't know what's happening in that tiny brain of yours? You're imagining a nice little scene where you can save your little friend aren't you? I say friend... is that all he was to you Jack?"

He tilts his head to one side, mocking. Even though I've just returned from the toilets I feel the need to urinate again. I hadn't even realised, but yes, the plan to save Brian in the next part of my dream did exist. I wanted something good to come out of the experience, and to know I'd actively tried to save him, not just considered it. In this constructed reality he might never die.

The man leans over the table, sips at his whisky chaser and places it back on a beermat. He whispers, and I involuntarily lean in too, to hear him.

"Interesting that you think of saving him rather than your own family... your own flesh and blood... your own living flesh and blood... what if you didn't get the chance though Jack? What if you didn't get the chance to even see him... what if this isn't all about you? Can I tell you a secret Jack, can I tell you what you really are?"

His voice drops a register and a notch on the volume control, and I lean in closer. I'm drawn in by him. I really do want to know what he thinks I am. And I know I'll totally believe whatever he tells me.

"What am I?"

That's when his fist hits the bridge of my nose with a loud cracking noise. The last thing I remember is him shaking his knuckles in annoyance, and cradling his own hand.

"Shit... that fucking hurt... I'm almost as stupid as you are... thumb outside the bloody fist, isn't it? I think I fucking broke it..."

FOUR – 17th October 1964

It's slightly less disconcerting this time. I know from before I open my eyes that I'm not in the same location. Not in the pub, not in the cemetery gardens, and not in my flat. It smells different to any of those. I'm not a hundred percent certain why I'd thought of those three places first, but I had. There is a soft breeze on my face. I reach up and gently test the back of my head for lumps. Pleasingly, there are none. Good sign. I touch my nose even more tentatively, but find it neither broken nor bloody. I'm unsure why I do either of those two things but it seemed important to check them, like something might have happened to my face or head recently.

I keep my eyes closed and inhale deeply again. I quite like the idea of not looking, so I wait. I breathe. I wait a while longer, content in the dark behind my eyelids. Some memories drift back to me. Not all, but enough. Wherever my imagination has taken me this time, it's better than that pub and having unwelcome thoughts and predictions pushed on me. I frown. I don't know what unwelcome thoughts or predictions I'm referring to. Something clearly hasn't gone well. Something is wrong, or I wouldn't be feeling this so strongly. I strain to try and put it all back together again, but my most recent memories remain just out of reach. I relax my face. Which brings back another unpleasant suspicion that I've recently been hit. In my face. I reach up to my nose again, just to be sure, but it's fine.

This had happened last time, it will come back to me. My thoughts flit back and forth. What do I mean 'had happened last time'? What had happened? Something quite like this, I think. A lived memory. Being at a different point in time. I don't know all the details yet but I'm not scared. I retain the sense I've been through something like this strangeness before and so therefore I will again. One detail rings quite clearly in my mind. For some reason I have to talk to someone, I know that. I'm not sure who it is that I need to talk to, or why, but for whatever reason I'm convinced I need to complete a quest or something. Yes, I have to talk this time, that's it. Details are still muddy, but I have a fact and that is enough of a motivation to start, and is more than I'd had before, the last time this happened. I think. Step one of quest, open eyes.

It's green again (not quite sure why 'again' yet). This is good. I like green. Daylight. Slight sense of déjà vu, but not in a bad way. Why isn't there an

English word for déjà vu? Don't get distracted. Eyes open, task one accomplished. This is going to be a piece of piss.

I look around at my surroundings and know pretty much straight away where I am. Just to one side of me there stands a very distinctive toolshed, in the centre of what is obviously a garden square. I'm sat on a park bench, but this time with a different view, and a few hundred yards away from where I woke up the last time. The outline of my previous experiences this evening return to me. I glance around Falkner Square.

The Georgian houses poking through the trees confirm my assumption, and I sit for a moment longer, composing myself. It's bitterly cold, and I pull the donkey jacket tighter across my chest, microseconds before registering that I'm wearing a donkey jacket. And a hat. A cap of some sort. I just accept those facts for the moment, standing and stamping my feet. The grass is long and the bushes unkempt. I take a few paces forward for a better view through the trees. The house in front of me looks empty, boarded up, the front garden overgrown. A familiar word, 'tatty', springs to mind and seems to understate the view.

The gardens are empty apart from me, and the gates shut and locked. I walk around over the grass, looking round for clues but don't find any. The problem with this part of Town is that it is almost two hundred years old, and hasn't changed much in terms of buildings, which is why it's so popular with TV crews making historical dramas. No clues apart from the sense of dilapidation, which rules out the present day when it's finally been tarted up a bit, but it could still easily be anytime in the last hundred and fifty years. I accept the fact this would be a different time as read, with sufficient knowledge of my experiences earlier in the evening (evening? It seems to be afternoon) to grasp what's going on, and confident enough to accept whatever this part of my ongoing dream throws at me. The dream, of course. More gaps fill in.

The lack of people doesn't help me to narrow down the date any more. The quiet roads seem quite similar to the early weeks of the pandemic a few years back, a period of weirdly empty streets. So maybe this is one of the wartimes? One of the things I did know about these old houses was that they'd been built by the wealthy and great, back when Liverpool ruled the trading World in the early 1800's, but that very quickly they'd moved out of fashion, and by the turn of that century they'd been a shadow of their former selves, and soon became tenements and flats. I know my local history. They were refurbished and neat again in the present day, part of the post Capital of Culture revitalisation of the city, but that was a fairly recent event in the big scheme of things.

I look more carefully and see lampposts, electric, so it must be twentieth century. Parts of the jigsaw come together. I don't like jigsaws, but I do like figuring things out, taking evidence and facts and working out how they go together. It has always been a bit of an aptitude I had, which would explain why I'd fallen into a job where you could follow logic and find solutions, testing and developing your methods as you went. The repairing and even the building of computers had appealed to me and had come so simply, which is why I'd started working in them. I like easy and I'd liked being able to fix and solve things. It gave a wonderful sense of achievement. Discovering everything about computers followed from very basic principles had led me into working on websites and that had been easy too. Applying the same logical approach to unfamiliar surroundings when you're suddenly dumped into them isn't so straightforward. A lot of the basic knowledge I need for assumptions is missing from my brain, but electric street lighting is one clear and undeniable indication I'm no further back than the twentieth century.

Assuming this is the past of course. It suddenly strikes me that there's no reason this can't be the future that I'm in; a World gone to ruin. I've had my spectral visits from Liverpool past and present, maybe this is Liverpool future? Aliens or zombies have taken over. Or another pandemic, a horribly possible scenario. I hop over the gate and walked to the corner, looking down towards the tower to see the Anglican Cathedral rising up impressively.

When I say I hop over the gate, that's how I'd like to present it to you. It's a fairly high gate and I'm sixty. I tried to open it a dozen times, then scrambled awkwardly, catching my jacket, then my trousers, shifting position when I'd realised my hip wouldn't open to the degree I needed. Let's just say I made it over mostly in one piece. Eventually. Then I bent over, panting. I stayed like that for several minutes, one hand on the railings in case I needed support getting upright again. It was a fucking stupid thing to try and do. I'm not as young as I used to be. Not that I had much choice unless I wanted to remain in the gardens indefinitely. Why the gates were locked remains a mystery. They're public gardens.

Anyway, eventually, after much panting, I walk over to the corner of the road, and the Anglican Cathedral rises up at the bottom of the hill like I said. The top of it pokes out anyway. It tells me nothing useful. I know that the Cathedral wasn't completely finished until the late seventies, but the bulk of it had been finished a lot earlier so the view is useless for dating.

I only notice the parked cars then, ugly, cheap, a lot of pastel colours, and mostly belonging in a scrapyard. The momentary quiet I'd experienced is over as first one moving car, and then a steady stream of other old cars come up the street and past me, one belching out a foul smelling grey smoke. I'd call them vintage except that implies something of value, and these are pieces of shit. I'm not a big car man, but they don't look like eighties or even seventies models. The identity of the present year is narrowing itself down for me.

A round fronted bread van drives past, and I'm reminded more of the things you see in Pathé newsreels and fifties films. So not at all recent then. I'm still acclimatising to everything, so only now put my hands into my trouser pockets, which are of what seems like canvas or similar brown material I note, in order to see what might be there. Nothing but lint in the pockets. I look down at dark brown boots. That doesn't help me understand much, boots are boots. I reach into my donkey jacket, not expecting my phone this time, but I'm pleased to find a wallet. A fairly smart, brown leather one. I open it hoping for more clues, but don't find any beyond the money inside. Then again, money is always good. Two old fashioned one pound notes and a couple of ten Bob ones. I stare at them, fascinated. I'd been born in '63 so the imperial money isn't totally alien to me, fortunately. And there seems to be a fair bit of it there.

I carry on over to Falkner Street, the adjacent road. Instantly, I can see how much worse this street has fared than the ones around the Square. Completely derelict buildings, buildings totally missing from the terraces, places bombed out and never replaced or rebuilt. I glance up at the sky, whether expecting to see German planes I don't know, but I do a quick calculation to try and put clues together as another old fashioned and very round fronted car splutters past. It isn't a newly purchased car by any means, not from a showroom, so given the shelf life of automobiles, from the little I know, the year couldn't be too early or too late in the century. I ponder further as I shuffle around the corner. The currency I have meant this is before the seventies, the housing damage suggests after the war, but maybe not by much. I might not even have been born yet. That's a peculiar proposition. Obviously having been bubbling under my observations and conclusions, a more relevant question pops up. One that seemed very familiar in its basic premise. What the fuck am I doing in the nineteen fifties? I won't know anyone, so what can I be expected to do here?

A little wave of memory laps gently over my conscious brain, an image of two men in a pub, one older, dressed like I usually do, bloody nose. One younger, seeming to enjoy the discomfort on his drinking partner's face. Why? What does that image mean? For some reason I still have a crystal clear certainty that there had been a phone call with Shelly which had started all this strangeness, though I still don't know what it had been about. More of my evening is dribbling back again bit by bit, which is a positive.

Half a dozen cars whizz past me in either direction, buzzing little disruptions to my mental un-fracturing. Surely there should be less traffic in the past, not more? But, if it really is the fifties... I perk up, sweeping aside all my worries from a second ago. This could be amazing. I may not have been born in this time, but this would be before Liverpool got big, and I know just enough of the history to know who was around in the City, and where and when. If this was the right year... I could actually meet the Beatles before they made it, meet Lennon himself. I don't like the fucker, think he was an over-rated prick in fact, and by the accounts I've read, a bit of a cock and twice as much a mardy bastard, but fuck that, I could meet him just the same! And talented famous people too. This was the era when footballers took the bus and drank in the local. I think, unless that's just a rose tinted past being peddled by newspapers and talking heads TV programmes. I can't recall anyone very famous from our two teams back in the fifties. I can't name many famous footballers anyway, not really my thing. Stanley Matthews and Dixie Dean. And Emlyn Hughes, Kenny Dalgleish. I don't know what I'd say to a footballer either. Well done, you can kick a ball between two sticks? The poets and writers I'd heard of, I don't think would be famous yet. My momentary reverie fades. Even if this was the end of the fifties the Beatles would still be kids, and I'd be a sixty year old stalking what would be at best, teenagers. Not a good look. Not even in the fifties.

I turn swiftly away from the city centre and head up towards Crown Street, away from Town. I'm determined to get something positive out of this experience if it kills me, and all my other ideas so far have been shit. Even if I wasn't born yet in this time, I know I can get a real thrill out of one thing. As a kid we'd cross Parliament Street and head over to the goods yard of Crown Street railway station, play in the coal trucks and see how close to the tunnels we could creep before we got chased off. Just once or twice, we made it right inside and that might sound like nothing, but I think they were some of my happiest memories of all. Me, Brian, Tank and numerous other lads at various times. Feeling brave, having fun, not a care in the world, and certainly not concerned about the fact that jumping across the tracks and in front of massive engines could have seen us crushed in seconds.

I'm aware I have a very silly smile on my face as I walk in that direction now, breathing in the different and familiar smell, but I don't care. I'm going to a good place. I can't pinpoint the exact mixture of aromas, but there's a definite edge of oil and tar to them, and ahead of me I can see the old court housing. Massive ring council estates, supposedly the future and forward looking but even fairly new, obviously a pen for the lucky ones displaced by slum clearance, out of the way of progress, packed together in high tech high-rise blocks. We'd alternated between envy of living in the huge hollow structures and laughing at the occupants who didn't have real houses like we did. They may not have been much, but they were our own, real houses. Well, the council's anyway. The kids from the estates would sometimes find us in the yards, sometimes joining in our games, but just as frequently chasing us off shouting how we were "shit in a buckets." I remember that insult vividly. I'm sure we didn't understand half of what we said, just mimicked our parents' words. I remember a particular time that one estate kid singled Brian out from the half-dozen of us playing, calling him a "darkie queer" and telling him to go "back home where he came from." It didn't even register at the time that the kid starting the trouble was a shade of brown himself. It was an insult designed to provoke us, so we let it do what it was designed for. We piled in en-masse.

We'd all got battered for a second time when we got home, bruised and bloody from fighting. I got the belt on my backside and legs, as much for losing the fight than anything else I suspect. My objections fell on deaf ears, until I mentioned the insult that started it all, and described the kid who shouted the insult out. My dad obviously knew who he was, and I guess the boy or his family had gained a reputation I didn't know about, for causing friction. A few of the dads from our street went out that night, and there were more than just kids with cuts and bruises the next morning. I was told in no uncertain terms to come straight home and tell Dad if that "Paki bastard" said anything again. Don't get me wrong, my dad wasn't an angel but he wasn't prejudiced by colour or race particularly. Not like that might sound to you now. No more prejudiced than anyone else was anyway. As a white family we were in the minority on our streets, but I think the epithet he used had a sharper ring to him than "Estate bastard". It was just an accepted term you could use. Something else that has changed a great deal in the intervening decades.

Thinking about episodes of my young life, I stand on the edge of the railway yard, taking in the vista of the tunnels and tracks and row after row of goods trucks. It's grass and a playground these days, exercise bars for adults too, only the big brick exhaust tower lets me know where I stand in relation to the area that I'm more recently familiar with. It's nice being here with the trucks and rails still where they should be. But playing on the tracks no longer appeals.

The rings of flats seem to loom as I look at them now, entrance arches facing me, trying to tempt me into going through. It's like an entrance to an underworld. A lot of these estates were called Farms. Ironic. Unless they meant battery farms.

I sigh sadly, the enjoyment of being here fading, not wanting to dwell on a time I can never get back, and knowing somewhere still just beyond my grasp is the reason I'm really here. I was remembering the young guy in the pub better now, not what he said exactly, but that he'd told me things. Things that may be useful to know now. I also remember that he hadn't seemed particularly helpful or friendly. I don't think that he'd told me anything about my phone call with Shelly, but I can't be certain. This acts as a jog to my memory about the last normal part of my life, the phone call itself.

I head down the street between the 'vision-of-the-future' concrete and brick structures which the future would rather forget. What the fuck had that conversation with Shelly been about? That gap in my knowledge seems to have been with me for hours. The blank frustrates me and pushes me to the verge of doubting it even happened. Even the 'normal' part of my life is in question. How could something which obviously affected me so much just vanish into vagueness? It happened before my seemingly lost hours, but I can't remember a single thing about it. Sarah? Had it been to do with Sarah? Was she going somewhere? Had she gone somewhere? Why else would I think of her name?

I'm not paying much attention to the streets themselves, or the traffic, or the people, beyond the detail they exist. Nothing stands out or strikes me enough to break my train of thought. Things are supposed to be so different in the past aren't they, but apart from small details of fashion it doesn't seem so very different? Apart from the hats, I notice. Far more people have hats, including me. I would have taken it off and thrown it away but it was doing a decent job at keeping my head warm. My hair isn't as insulating as when I was young.

With a sense of inevitability I enter a newsagent I spot, buy a newspaper and, once again, a packet of cigarettes and some Swan Vesta matches. Pall Mall cigarettes, the brand my father had smoked. These were the first ones that caught my eye. The man behind the counter hadn't been happy that I only had a note, but grudgingly found the change. I rolled the many coins in my hand, unfamiliar yet familiar, and put them back into my spacious trouser pocket. I'd look at them later.

The headline in the newspaper reads 'Wilson's Choice' and explains that Labour have just won the election. I deliberately don't look at the date first, and try to guess the exact year just for shits and giggles, but the headline means my assumption of 1955 must be well out. Martin Luther King Jr has apparently been awarded a Nobel Peace Prize. Cole Porter has just died. I don't want to read any further. None of it would be 'news' to me, just history. I read the front cover again. It's still 17th October, but this time it's a Saturday, in 1964.

1964. I must be just over a year old, somewhere out there in the city. That is a weird prospect. I want to have the urge to go and see my family, to see myself, to see my parents still alive, but I find the idea quite unappealing in reality. I leave the shop and mosey in the same direction I had been going before, paper under my arm as I don't have any pockets big enough. This time I intend to head straight to Town. I know that I'm supposed to talk to people, I'm fairly certain that is my prime directive I have to complete, though I'm not sure what the completion of this task will result in.

It's still early, on a Saturday as I now know, so there will be crowds in the city centre, and enough space to acclimatise for a while before I'll need to make the effort to converse. I surprise myself by how calm and accepting I am about it all, and the conviction I have this mysterious quest to complete. I'm here, and let things fall where they may. And I'm going to die in a few hours. This crucial detail of knowledge comes back to me very suddenly, but oddly it doesn't seem as concerning to me now. It's still a dream I'm in, isn't it? I'm not sure which specific parts of it I want to take seriously, but the predictions of a stranger (who I now have the distinct impression I didn't like) aren't going to worry me unduly. I reach absently up to the bridge of my nose and stroke it. I drop the unread newspaper into the first bin I pass.

I stand stock still as, like a massive spider, the skeleton of the Catholic Cathedral looms up in front of me and takes my breath away. It seems so much bigger than the finished article, and a huge crane is nestled snugly in the middle, its upper beams half hidden by scaffolding, nothing more than a shell of concrete and steel girders. More than anything so far, this drives home to me the changes to when I am. I'd been too young to remember the cathedral being built and it existed in its entirety as a finished article from as early as I remember. Seeing it half built is almost as creepy as it is impressive.

I slowly edge my way forward again, making my way towards the immense building, subsumed with awe. I'm not a Catholic, or even religious, but it's hugely impressive this close up, and partway through its birth. The last time I'd felt like this was when I'd visited the Anglican one as it was being finished, in the late seventies. That one was much bigger of course, and more traditional, but this was somehow better. Like a church in its underwear. I headed as close as I could without the corrugated fence cutting off my view, and see a couple of men muttering and desperately scrubbing red paint off the fence. 'God's own house for the Christians, Paddy's heathen's get a wigwam'. Charming.

Someone was brave to risk writing that in plain sight. Religion back in the sixties is still, well, like a religion I suppose. And desecrating somewhere like this, even un-consecrated, is like declaring war on half of the city. Catholic and Protestant had never been a particular issue that I remembered from my own neighbourhood, important of course, but not really an issue or source of many big conflicts. With so many different faiths and backgrounds mixing, there was a natural tolerance of others in the vicinity of your own house, you couldn't afford to be otherwise. I know it was very different down in places like Scotland Road though, the Irish and Scots' issues still going on today had been fought in the slums and in the tight, packed communities by the docks. Religion trumped race as the great divider down there. Through the following decades 'Paddy's Wigwam' would later become an almost affectionate name for this cathedral, barely causing consternation, and very little genuine offence, until the most recent decade when again, it had become a taboo reference, as being disrespectful.

I could hear the man with the scrapers and whitewash angrily talking about the "Proddy bastards" and what would happen when he found them, and I saw a second even worse daubing just beyond, bleeding back through the white paint already. The spelling was poor, but the vandals had added that 'The bishop of rome sucks culloreds', clearly designed to cause as much offence as possible in a few words. I doubted it had been kids, they wouldn't have had the nerve, more likely one of the gangs looking to provoke a fight. If many people had seen these words then they would probably get their way.

"What do you think you're looking at? Go on, piss off!"

I'm quite surprised to find that shout aimed at me. I scuttle off before remembering I'm in my sixties, and shouldn't be receiving such disrespectful abuse. Though if they thought I was Anglican and gloating, or might tell others about it, perhaps I just got off lightly. Disrespectful? Had I really just thought that word? You have to be respectable to be disrespected. Smoking the frankly disgusting Pall Mall, I head down into Town itself, enjoying the sight of the dark green and cream bus going past as it reminds me of happier, if, it seems not simpler, times. Happier if you were a kid, I think.

#

The City Centre is a genuine revelation. You can instantly tell the difference in almost everything here, the noise, the smell, the traffic, the woman smacking her kid in the street. I'd still hung on to the idea that there were supposed to be more cars in modern days, but I'd forgotten everything is so pedestrianised in my world, and that this is a relatively recent addition in the big scheme. Church Street, the main shopping street, is insanely busy with both cars and people, though I suppose it being a Saturday that shouldn't be unexpected. Woolworth's, C and A, Marks and Spencer, many of the brands are familiar though the logos of those surviving are different, and the smallest changes resonate with me, though the number of hats and headscarves is still the biggest. It doesn't look like the swinging sixties you hear about, and re-affirms my belief that is all retrospective PR. Much as today, there are a few people in outlandish clothes and clearly statement outfits, but I think they'd be more shocked at what we wear now. Another odd realisation hits me, the lack of jeans on men, and the fact men who are presumably only my actual age looked well beyond that, like they want to be appear old, and had chosen their look on what they thought old men should wear.

I wander into a few shops, browsing, remembering I'm supposed to be engaging with people, even if I still don't recall exactly why. The remaining gaps in memory are really bugging me by now. And I'm discovering that striking up conversations isn't as easy as I imagined, not if friendliness doesn't come naturally to you, like it doesn't to me. Particularly when you have no idea who you're supposed to be talking to, or what about. I have a few short conversations with random people, but the bustle and lack of engagement is exactly as it would be today. You don't just chit chat with a stranger for no reason.

These people all around me would be the parents' generation I remembered, the aunties and uncles.

That is my thought while I pause at the traffic lights, and even if I don't recognise them, it could be my own ancestors and relatives walking past me every second. My next thought, following almost immediately, is that it probably wouldn't be. Even though Town was so near to where we lived, I don't remember my mother or father venturing into the city centre much, unless there was a specific need, for 'start of school clothes' or Christmas. Window shopping wasn't something they did, had the time, money or inclination for. I stand outside Woolies for a few minutes, basking in the window display and things I haven't seen for decades, then wander aimlessly further along the street before I turn about and head back up towards what seemed more like home. To be frank, I feel a little lost and out of place this far from my comfort zone.

Bold Street looks roughly the same as the one I know, which is helpful, but glancing left or right along Hanover Street at the bottom of it is very peculiar. Seeing an overground railway station other than Lime Street is jarring. I light yet another cigarette (it's the sixties so chain smoking is allowed before you comment on my addiction) and unsurprisingly decide I need a drink. I can see a Yates's Wine Lodge on the corner, just beyond the station, and that will serve two purposes, primarily alcohol, but also this is the kind of place people talk, loudly, whether you wanted them to or not.

The fug of smoke that washes over me as I enter hits me like a wall, even though I have a cigarette in my own mouth at the time. It's busy and loud inside, but there's plenty of space. I move just behind two pretty young women, admiring their dresses. Okay, admiring what's in them. One has a dark blue polka dot dress, alice band and long dark hair, the other a plain navy dress. Even in the modest fashions they have on, they clearly have good figures, and lovely tits that should have been set free into the wild rather than languishing under tight fabric. You can sometimes just tell, whatever a girl wears, and I'm a little jealous of the man receiving their attentions. They're giggling and affecting the posh unconvincing Scouse accent you try and put on when you're trying to impress, as the young man opposite tries his luck. His dark skin and West Indian accent make him stand out, but he's clearly trying to use that to his own advantage, hinting at exotic tales of his travels on various ships, and how important he seemingly is to the whole merchant navy. I suspect he may be as full of shit as I was at his age, but the girls are lapping it up so he gets my grudging respect for that.

I order a beer, tentatively picking out some coins rather than a note, and hope a shilling and six will do it, not having bought beer in the period, and with no prices in obvious sight. It seems I'm not far off, and I move to stand by a high table and take in the room, settle myself, and think. Decide what it might be that I was supposed to know, actually do, or find out, and maybe put together the last pieces of missing memory about that dick in the leather coat.

Instead, a mental image of Brian comes back to me, in his red hoodie, looking like he wants to tell me something. Lips moving but no words coming out. I close my eyes for a minute to concentrate, and try and lip-read what I'm imagining, not that it helps me. He seems to be tied into everything that is happening to me in some fashion, but whatever I was going to get out of this dream, it can't be directly to do with him, not in 1964. Brian was a couple of years younger than me, and he wouldn't even have been born yet. I picture my mother instead, but the picture I get is of her with a baby on the tit, which, despite the fact it would have been me suckling, no man wants to see. I try to think of my father instead, but even though I knew his face so well for so many years, it won't come into focus. Whether this is part of my brain telling me I'm on the wrong track, or whether in the absence of keeping any photographs I've forgotten exactly what he looked like, I can't tell. I try to think if I'd ever heard them talk about anything which might have happened when I was a one year old, any event or significant happening which might be a flag indicating what I need to look out for. But if I once knew of anything, it isn't going to reveal itself to me now. The beer is stale, or maybe that's the smell of years of smoke and ashtrays. It doesn't stop me drinking more.

Listen. I'm supposed to listen. Not to talk. That revelation is like a huge weight lifted. Every tiny detail I know or recall seems like a surreal clue in a massive bastard jigsaw of my life, without a picture to refer to. So it's a case of trying every shape in every hole. Would anything happen if I had sex here? Could I father a child? Don't know why that comes to mind but the likelihood of me getting the opportunity seems remote anyway. In the films, with time travel it's always killing your own grandfather, or becoming your own father, something like that. Neither is likely in this scenario. Grandad Bert was already dead, heart attack before I was born. And I'm already alive here. Shit, am I meant to be Brian's father? I don't linger on that one for too long. It's true his dad wasn't around by the time Brian was growing up, but I've seen photographs. And the idea of me sleeping with Mrs Touré (even now I can't use her given name) scares the fuck out of me. She was never what you'd describe as soft. And the idea of her giving it up to a sixty year old white man was ludicrous. I push the whole subject aside before I started imagining it in detail.

There's a saying that people can smell danger. Unless it's the smell of a lion, I don't think that's true, but sometimes you can definitely sense an impending situation, the small hairs on the back of your neck rising is the clichéd description, but as I drank quietly at my table, lost in thought, it seemed like the voices around me were getting louder. It started innocently enough.

A few feet away three loud young bucks, as I think this time would describe them, are clearly the worse for wear, and are having, well, I wouldn't call it a conversation as there was only one voice leading whatever was said. At the centre of the crowd is a tall, tanned figure with carefully styled hair, a crisp yellow shirt, brown tie, sports jacket and high-waisted tan trousers and belt. I can't place the accent beyond somewhere in the Southern states of America, but he's clearly very well off, and has that sense of entitlement you get from people who've never had to work a day in their lives and don't really understand the concept. I don't know why I hadn't noticed him before because he sticks out like a sore thumb, and is blatantly used not only to being the focus of attention, but revels in it. With him are two other figures, one short, stocky and tanned, also smartly dressed in a jacket and tie but almost deliberately with a touch less colour or style, and a brick shithouse in one of those college Jock jackets you see in movies, blonde hair in less of a style than a mop, and a dopey grin on his face. They sound American to me too, but I'm not great at accents so I couldn't tell you where from. My first impression of them is of the Malfoy kid in the Harry Potter films, with his two dumb stooges to back him up.

"Don't try to be funny Todd, you don't have the intellect. You're only here because I needed someone who could drive, and I can always send you back on the next plane home."

Todd is obviously the short one, and the tall gormless one guffaws as though this is the funniest thing anyone has ever said. Todd just accepts it weakly, forcing a smile himself to join in.

"Whatever you say Don, you're the chief..."

This 'Don' accepts what he takes to be an apology.

"Not yet, but I will be soon. Four more weeks of this and I'll be close. Father is giving me one of the Wells outside Jackson for graduation, and I finally get to show what I can do..."

There are murmurs of approval and, well, arse-licking I guess and Don, his beaky nose giving him a striking profile, swigs down a beer and glances about him, clearly hoping for admiring glances from others in the pub too. All he gets are dismissive looks for talking so loudly.

"I know the Adelphi isn't what you're used to Donny, but at least you're treated with the respect you deserve there..."

This is the short one, Todd, climbing even further up his neighbour's arse, and drunk enough to assume that namedropping will impress anyone in listening distance too. Not only drunk, but definitely not very bright, and certainly not a good judge of the wider audience. I never catch the name of the third one, but he seems to be mainly there to nod and laugh. I think it's an off colour joke that provokes the first really raucous gale of laughter from him after that, followed by something I don't catch about long hair and queers. I've heard plenty of raw conversation and jokes since I've been back in the sixties, but because the boys themselves stick out by the virtue of their look and accents, their conversation draws attention more than others. I get the distinct impression that this Don is slumming it slightly in Yates's, showing off for his entourage how he can fit in and be admired anywhere, and I don't think I'm the only one making that interpretation. I think it might have been the subtle change in stance, or occasional glances they were getting from various quarters that alerts me to the fact that trouble is brewing. The people surrounding us clearly aren't impressed, and the loud banter is veering into the territory that annoys other patrons more significantly.

The leader of their pack glances towards the bar, and I realise from something about his look that he'd turned in that direction several times before in the last few minutes as well. That might have been what I'd picked up on in first sensing genuine trouble brewing. The subject of his scrutiny is glaringly obvious.

Only a few feet away are the girls I'd been admiring myself, and the merchant sailor chatting them up, his own yellow shirt and chino's an ironic mirror of those worn by Donny. It doesn't take a genius to work out that his skin colour is the primary reason for the attention the Americans are now paying him. The silence between jokes allows his accent to float forth more distinctly, offering another drink to both of the girls. If I had to guess I'd say Jamaican, but like I said, accents aren't my strong point.

It's almost like watching pack animals. Todd and the jock follow the leader's gaze, and then look at each other and back at their friend, waiting for what comes next, ready to jump on board and back up what they clearly know is on its way. The threesome at the bar themselves are oblivious, lost in their own world of flirtation, but I can sense I'm not the only one picking up on the rapidly changing vibe.

Donald slowly lights his own cigarette, flashing his Zippo lighter ostentatiously, and the volume of his voice clearly rises a deliberate notch.

"I thought this town was supposed to be more civilised you know boys... back in the war they were big supporters of the right side... my Grandpa always used to tell about some of the fine folk of Liverpool who came to visit and help the cause when he was young, like minded they were, recognised what it meant to be... properly civilised... but it seems that standards are slipping since then... never mind the ridiculous ideas back home, it's more 'Civilised Rights' we need! "

By the immediate and almost automatic reaction of his buddies, I'm guessing this isn't the first time Don has made this 'joke'. He carries on, completely oblivious to the fact he's drawing more and more attention with every loud new word, and not the appreciative attention he seems to believe he would get. I almost will him to stop, knowing I was a prick when I was young too, and when I was drunk often believed everyone would agree with whatever I said or thought because I was smart. I almost willed him. Another part of me was waiting to see where this might lead and if he'd get battered. That wouldn't upset me too much.

I knew from listening to stories when I was growing up that Americans weren't always popular in this period, and the war he was talking about clearly wasn't the one many of the people around me would have recently served in, more the American Civil one, which is a highly inappropriate name for it too (see, that's a genuinely funny pun on the word 'civil'). While behind scouse pub walls, we might criticise ourselves amongst ourselves with immunity, everyone knows that much of the city's wealth has come from trade with the plantations and southern states, and we don't like or need reminding of that at the best of times, particularly by outsiders. Certainly not these outsiders. And we're a port city, not some backwater, we know what happens elsewhere in the World, and we move with the changing times. That was my thinking on the rising levels of irritation in the other drinkers, but it might just have been that these three were annoying little dicks. And it's never a good idea to insult a place you're drinking in anyway, of course. Particularly this one, which isn't the most salubrious of venues. Yates's 'Wine Lodge'. Sounds almost like a country club. If you've ever been in a Yates's you'll appreciate the irony of that.

Don's supporting cast bob their heads and mutter approval and agreement on the bond Liverpool shared with the American south, and that

Liverpudlians would want to rectify any slipping of standards he'd been talking about. Not living up to the morals and viewpoint of the deep south was an oversight no doubt, and everyone here would be grateful for having it pointed out. All three are drunk enough that whatever common sense or awareness they might have once had is long since gone.

"I know we've got to watch out for Reds these days, but the other... colours... sneak their way in everywhere too... polluting places... not knowing their place..."

"The end of a rope?"

There's a twisted, gurning grin on the shorter one, head tilted upwards giving away the need for approval. A half spat out drink through a laugh shows he has it, and the tall blonde one follows with a cursory glance and required additional bark of laughter. Don may have been marginally more intelligent than the other two, as he pretended that was just a weak joke, and that he was far more reasonable than that level of open bigotry. Self-awareness clearly isn't his strongest suit.

"No Todd, be reasonable now... those days are gone... a shame, but there you go, the World has changed... but that's no reason to let standards slip... so long as they keep to their own... they can even be good little workers... we have a few on the sites...

ugly as sin and dumb as pigs, but they have something to give... when they accept their place... with their own... not making fools of themselves in front of their betters, and not scaring pretty young things they shouldn't even have the nerve to stand near..."

He looks pointedly over towards the bar as conversation around falls a little quieter, and the sense of impending danger rises.

"Say Don... didn't your great grandpa own some of them?"

"Some? We had one of the biggest estates in all Louisiana... those were the days... we were born too late boys... back before the Pinkos and the liberals interfered..."

They clink pint glasses, toasting a particular past and at the same time congratulating themselves on being rich, redneck or not. The toast just seems to encourage them to push the direction of conversation further, and I think everyone in listening distance can tell where it's ultimately headed. Apart from the three at the bar, who are still chatting away, oblivious. The two loud goons spend several minutes getting more and more animated about the 'good old days', taking their lead from the mood of the rich kid, and bit by bit, work more insults and anger into their own little conversation, building themselves up, needing to find a place they could use to work out some drunken aggression. Impressing those around seems forgotten as an aim, and as one they all turn their heads slightly so the volume of their comments was directed straight at the bar.

"Did you own lots of them, Donny?"

It was the first thing I'd heard the jock say, his low voice as slow as his brain might be, though he manages to frame it in a way that gives his friend credit for owning and running a plantation himself, instead of his great grandfather.

"Dozens, hundreds probably... we ran the place with a rod of iron, firm but fair, one of the best in the State..."

Don smiles, accepting that credit for himself now, like he alone had been in charge of running the long-gone slave estate, rather than him being someone who's ancestors had made their money in cotton. And by what he's said earlier, rather than being the fortunate son of a family who'd apparently gone on to strike it lucky with oil and regain their fortune. With another glance, he's clearly building himself up to approach the subject of his ire more directly. The short little arse licker picks up on the look, and takes it upon himself to provide the launching platform.

"They must have had lots of kids... they can't help breeding... you think anyone here is related to any of the ones you owned?"

The conversations all around have hushed totally by now, and the three at the bar have finally noticed. The two women are looking uncomfortable and inching away.

"Doubt it... we trained our niggers proper... none of them would dare speak to a white woman... they knew what would happen to them..."

And there it was. The West Indian turns to look over at them, clearly pissed off, but just as clearly not surprised, and sober enough himself, and with more sense than to call out three pissed-up bigots directly. But his look back over at them is the opportunity which they've been looking and hoping for.

"What are you looking at, boy?"

Bolstered by his own talk, the need to show off, and the alcohol, Donald pushes back his stool and stands, wobbling slightly. This is his big moment to impress.

"Don't you dare look me in the eye, nigger... you filthy... coon scum..."

It wasn't exactly eloquent, witty, or anything other than an excuse to insult. And intimidate. Another barstool scrapes back though, and a deep, rumbling Scouse voice butts in.

"Are you calling me a nigger, son? 'Cos I'm the one who's looking you in your shifty little eyes..."

Confusion and annoyance flash in the American's expression as he takes in the sight of the large, fifty plus year-old Scouser with a huge beard who is now standing in his path.

"Out of the way grandpa... I'm talking to the nig..."

Have you ever seen a Hollywood film where furniture seems to be made of balsa wood? A second after the thud of a large folded fist cracks against the thin, now broken nose, the barstool and table crack themselves, and break apart loudly under the weight of the body thrown back against them. Bottles and glasses fly everywhere.

"I warned you not to call me that, lad... you're not with your Alabama buddies any more..."

After a moment frozen in time everything seems to happen at once. As a dazed figure on the floor shakes his head to clear it, his two drunk friends step forwards, as do half a dozen locals nearby. I've stayed on my stool, but as the people in front of me move I notice the figure on the floor wipe the blood from his nose, look at the fresh red stain on his hand, and reach out for a bottle of brown beer, broken off at the neck and rolling beside him.

I don't need to move quickly or far, but without thinking I stand and stamp my boot heavily down on his wrist, holding it there as he whips his head round to glare up at me with venom in his eyes. I return the look without flinching. There are rules to this kind of thing.

"Not inside Davey... not inside..."

A nervous man is moving out from behind the bar, clearly used to trouble but more concerned over his fixtures and fittings than anything else.

Todd and the jock pause as they square up, glancing nervously around and realising they aren't just slightly outnumbered, but totally in the shit. As big as one of them is, and as drunk, it's clear they aren't going to come out of this well if they try fighting. A myriad of expressions pass before the big American's eyes. Slow, but methodical. A fight wouldn't worry him, but he was clearly there to protect the Donald kid, and he wasn't doing a very good job so far. And it might actually make matters worse if he hits back. The thick, rumbling accent rolls over the bar again.

"Now why don't you just fuck off right now, like good little dickheads, and take that bag of Klan shit with you..."

No-one moves for a moment, and then, eyes flicking around the crowd to check for immediate threats, the two of them reach down to help their bloodied friend to his feet. I leave it an extra moment before removing my boot from his wrist, as a little message that they aren't out of the woods yet. Donald slaps away the proffered hands of his 'friends' and awkwardly rises to his feet, rubbing the wrist I'd been standing on.

He spits on the floor and his own eyes dart about anxiously. He doesn't want to catch the eye of anyone who might hit him again, and you can almost see the cogs whirring with the reluctant knowledge that looking directly towards the West Indian again would be a bad idea as well, if he wants to stay unpunched. His eyes settle on me, old and determined by him to be the least threatening. I'll suffice for him to make a gesture, and my restraint in doing no more than holding his hand down suggests he's going to be relatively safe aiming his resentment at me. He obviously isn't quite as stupid as he looks. I let him scowl at me, then see him hesitate as I accept and keep his gaze, not backing down, and giving him the choice of trying to make something of it, or breaking the connection first and leaving. He chooses the latter, the two others trailing after him, no doubt to be blamed themselves later. It's like a wild west tumbleweed moment until the door slams behind them, a futile and slightly petulant exit to make a point, and the silence is broken by that big rumbling Scouse laugh again.

"Little pricks... can't take their ale!"

It isn't funny, but that clearly doesn't matter and laughter ripples round the bar as people turn back to their seats. The object of the abuse seems largely forgotten, his female companions having abandoned him so I move forward and ask him if he's ok.

His eyes raise to mine and he tells me, his own accent thickening, that he doesn't need no help from me. It's an automatic switch we all do in situations like this, you either go to joking and dismissive mode, as Davey the local had, or defensive and wary if you're not sure whether the problems are over, like my reluctant friend here. I hadn't realised that the main defender and keeper of the peace had moved his large frame up beside me, jovial and only slightly drunk, but I think also wanting to make sure everything is okay and over too.

"He wasn't offering son... we don't give a fuck about you, don't know you... but we hate the Yankee bastards, thinking they own the place and they don't get to decide what happens here..."

"Yankees are northern, they were from the south I think..."

It comes out of my mouth automatically without me thinking, my innate pedantry coming out. The big, bearded face half turns towards me.

"Fuck off..."

It isn't unfriendly as such, but I take it as the warning it's obviously intended to be, not to comment anything further about what he says. As part of the crowd, with a local accent, I've been accepted, but not enough to have a voice of my own. He inclines his head over to where the barman is clearing the debris of the table and chair. And gives me a grudging compliment.

"Nice one though, with the bottle ..."

I didn't know he'd seen but should have known he would have. Clearly the veteran of more than one altercation, and thinking back, actually very restrained himself in the recent encounter, he'd also used the minimum of violence needed, just one persuasive punch. Davey clearly understood and appreciated that I'd done the same as him, in what could easily have escalated into a full-on brawl. As one-sided as it might have been. I doubt he'd have had much trouble if it had kicked off, but it was early evening and this was clearly his local, and not the time for a needless fight, with what he must have judged to be a minor irritation rather than a genuine problem. I nod and turn back to the Jamaican at the bar.

"You might want to think about leaving though, friend..."

Both sets of eyes swing back to me sharply, one set hostile and assuming I don't want him there, the other sharply observant to see where I'm going with my comment.

"I've the same right to be here as you, Mister..."

Now that the girls have gone, his strong accent suddenly fades too, and he talks in an almost clipped and RP tone, just a hint of the Jamaican lilt left. He obviously thinks his own regular accent will be more effective if I'm questioning his right to belong. Davey butts back in.

"You're not thinking about those little shits are you, lad? Trust me, we can handle a couple of pissants like that no trouble."

I light a cigarette, deliberately offering one each to them, which they take, a peace offering accepted. I don't take offence at the 'lad', even though he's years younger than me, that isn't what it means.

"I know we can..." (it was a deliberate use of 'we') "but I doubt they'd have the bollocks to do that, or be stupid enough... even dumb Yankees aren't that thick..." I picked the use of 'Yankees' deliberately this time as it seemed a good idea, and an easy way to appease the big man. "...but they look the type to try and find some likeminded souls...or pay some... then wait somewhere far enough away, down a sidestreet?" I pause for my meaning to sink in. "...Watch, trying to show they're real men... wait for him to leave on his own later... wait near a back street two of them can pull him into... unless you've got a load of mates here somewhere?"

I address the first part to Davey as I think he needed mollifying more, and then directly to the man who's evening and chances of that particular female company have now been pretty much ruined. I can see comprehension dawn on both their faces, and with a pinched expression, the Merchant Seaman licks his lips and slowly shakes his head that he doesn't.

"Fair enuff..."

Davey turns and drifts away, satisfied I'm not a threat or in danger of causing more trouble, and the West Indian at the bar pauses and almost nods at me, accepting my point, and turning back to what remains of his pint. He'd drink slowly enough to show he wasn't scared but fast enough to be able to leave before any ambush might be in place, or at least find some blokes he knows from his ship elsewhere. I return to my table where I still have beer waiting too.

#

I talked to a few people over the next hour, mainly meaningless chat as my acceptance by Davey, clearly one of the influencers here, means I'm judged to be okay. Then I'd raised a hand in acknowledgement to the big man and left, realising that my own warning about getting jumped and getting a kicking could equally apply to me. I might be sixty, but I'd played a prominent enough role in the trouble, and would be easy pickings for three or more pissed up and pissed off angry young men if I was on my own.

I decide to stick to the well- lit main streets as I amble out, with Bold Street, the shopping street heading up the hill and out of the city centre, offering me the most straightforward route away. I assume if there was to be further trouble it would be close by Yates's, and the areas back up by the Cathedrals are more familiar home ground to me anyway. I'm also getting hungry, and not wanting to brave a restaurant, am on the lookout for a chippy or a greasy spoon, which I assume will be my only other options for food. My heart is beating a little faster as I look back on what has just happened, and with the state of my heart that's never a very good sign. Perhaps a sit down to eat wouldn't be such a bad idea. It hadn't been an actual fight, and I was no stranger to scuffles if it had been, you couldn't be growing up here, but the words of the stranger in The Caledonia, back in my own time, and his prediction of my imminent demise come hurtling back at me. I'd been particularly stupid to get involved, even though I couldn't help myself. I automatically reach into my jacket for my phone to check the time, again forgetting my phone is long in the future. I check my wrist but whatever force had outfitted me for this period has omitted a watch again, which is rather a big omission.

Yes, I'm knocking on in years, have a heart condition, and am in a year with comparatively backward medical facilities, not knowing anyone who can take care of me. Joining in a potential fight had been monumentally stupid of me. Particularly when someone had recently predicted a heart attack for me in the coming hours, and without a watch or phone I don't know how many of those are still left.

Something catches the corner of my eye and in the back of my mind it makes a connection. I'm halfway up Bold Street, and there's a road to my right, Slater Street, which even in my day had boasted a version of the famous Jacaranda Club, or coffee bar as it would be now. It was famous. I was a few years too late to catch the Beatles performing there, but it would be interesting to see what it had been like, and I could have some food and a sit down there. I know I keep saying that the Beatles aren't a big thing for me, but you can't deny the history when you grow up in the city, and the chance to see a famous venue in its heyday is too much to pass up. My mind automatically wonders if there are any 'souvenirs' I might be able to liberate that could be valuable back in the present, but I doubt that is the reason I'm here, or if I can take anything back with me. It was strange, I'd finally accepted I was actually genuinely here at some point in the last hours, and not even realised the change in perception. If this was a dream it had become so vivid and credible that it may as well be real. So I should probably treat my time here like it actually is real. I count my money, finding I'm still pretty well off, and go inside.

#

I was getting more frustrated now. I'd talked to lots of different people; painful, awkward, dull conversations that struck home just how little I knew or remembered from the sixties, and how much everyday conversations include contemporary references and allusions. Perhaps fortunately, as an almost pensioner, I'd been excused knowledge of pop culture, music and film, though that is my strongest suit from this period. The war I'm sketchy on, but it hadn't come up that much, and my biggest problem was the recent news. Aside from the newspaper, which I'd only skimmed before binning, I had no idea what was current or important. I had a vague knowledge that things like the Profumo Affair had already happened, JFK would be dead, but knew very little about what else was happening in Britain, and even less about what was happening in Liverpool. And it seemed someone like me would be expected to know. Luckily, the people who'd talked to me had been more interested in the sound of their own voices than mine.

I was back on Hope Street by the cathedrals, having passed a very black and sooty looking Philharmonic pub, and decided against going in. Following my visit to The Jacaranda (where I'd been hugely out of place but had got by without too much trouble) I'd thought I may as well try another historic venue, one that wouldn't be too famous yet, and which was close to my heart as I'd drunk there on and off for years. The Philharmonic is just a passing temptation, not enough to make me stop.

I turn down the little side street instead, to head to a little hidden gem of a pub, Ye Cracke. I'm not certain on my exact dates, but while the musicians of Liverpool would have moved on from some of the local drinking places by now, the writers shouldn't have. And even later in the sixties, there were always apocryphal stories of the writers and painters who formed part of the Liverpool Scene, before it was even such a thing, congregating in this particular pub. I didn't know if I'd recognise them but it was worth a shot for the experience, and I liked the idea that whatever I was here to do or find out would involve at least a minor celebrity. Though mainly I just want another pint (the Jacaranda had been dry. How places managed to exist and thrive without a license was a mystery to me). I pull my jacket closed as the rain starts to spit down on me, and push the door open.

#

It hasn't changed at all really, or should that be wouldn't change at all really? Tenses are difficult when your present is your past, and your past is the future. On the outside it looks like a normal little pub, on the inside there's an attempt to create as many rooms in as small a space as possible; there's a lounge, a kind of snug, a backroom and a larger open space of a room with murals on the wall, plus the bar area itself. And most of these are crowded with half a dozen people in them. Comforting though. Compact and both chaotic and neat, if that makes any sense.

I decide on a pint of Mild to settle in, blinking my eyes against the smoke which congregates almost at head level. How did I ever used to find this normal when I went into a pub or club? Could have been the fumes already in my lungs. Unlike its more well-known counterparts like the Big House or the Philharmonic, this is a historic pub that has always pretty much kept the same clientele of just locals and those in the know. Nestled down an unobtrusive side street, and mispronounced by most, Ye Cracke has always been a meeting place for those from the surrounding area less interested in posing, though ironically many of its regulars over the years are those with the right to pose if they chose to. I wander around the different areas, not really expecting to see anyone famous, not least because of all the names I know that had drunk here around this time or earlier, I haven't got a clue what the fuck most of them looked like. Poets, painters, musicians, actors would mingle here, and while I like the romantic notion of it being a hotbed of artistic collaboration, to them it's just the pub. Yes, ideas would be swapped, people like the painter and tutor Arthur Ballard who would hold court, younger and newer drinkers hanging on the every word of those with the reputation, but mostly it's just an out of the way pub where likeminded individuals can congregate. And given its place in the mythos of Liverpool history, I guess that if there's anywhere I might hear, say, or do anything important, it might be here. I hope so. By now I'm getting fed up of talking to strangers for no reason and pretending to be interested in their bullshit.

It's fairly busy, being a Saturday evening, and I walk casually around with my pint, partly to see where there might be a seat, partly to see if I can identify anything I might be expected to take part in, or learn from. I've settled into an acceptance that if I'm definitely supposed to do something or hear something, I may as well embrace it and try properly. I had a brief interest in the fighting fantasy 'pick your own adventure' books forty years ago, even though I was a little old for them by that time. The idea of being able to choose where an adventure leads, and to take a hand in shaping and guiding my own narrative had appealed to me. As a young man, predating the computer games which would go on to be quite acceptable, doing it in a book meant I didn't have to risk ridicule for being a Dungeons and Dragons nerd. I can almost pretend this current location is one of those books. I just have to choose which group to join, and my adventure will be guided by that choice. It gives me a small sense of control which is very welcome.

Most areas are wall to wall with existing groups of acquaintances, so it's a choice of hanging by the bar or taking a seat by one of the tables in the far room. I choose the latter, despite the fact most of the interesting minor celebrity people will probably have chosen their own little private areas to hold court. The idea of a seat really appeals, it will give me the time to get the feel of the place and listen into as many conversations as I can to get my bearings, and try and decide what to do next. Which next step to pick.

No sooner have I sat down than a couple of young people follow my lead. Relatively smartly dressed, him in a brown suit and tie, her in a matching pink jacket and skirt. Slightly too dressy for a pub like this one.

"Is this seat taken?"

I have a mouthful of beer so incline my head, meaning it was free and they settle in beside me. I'd expected them to just take their places and chat together, but the guy holds his hand out to me instead.

"John..."

I grip his hand and shake. Let the conversation come to me.

"Jack..."

"This is Valerie..."

"Val..."

She holds out her own hand which was a bit unusual, but I shake it all the same. I'm determined to try and listen.

"We're quite new, I hope you don't mind us joining you? We only arrived in Liverpool a few weeks ago."

That explains the clothes which make them stand out, not being familiar with the usual dress code, or lack of it. I can't quite place his accent, but it's from

185

somewhere over the Pennines. All Creatures Great and Small type places maybe.

"We're working at the new theatre, have you been?"

"Volunteering..."

And quite desperate for friends it seems. They both have gin and tonics on the table, which doesn't help their blending in much.

"We met a few nice people already, but none of them seem t' be here yet... are you here with folk?"

I don't get the chance to answer the barrage of information as they barely pause for breath. The man at least seems aware of the fact and exchanges a look with the woman to see if she feels the same, that they're being a bit much. I take the opportunity to study his appearance. Oddly small mouth, neat and tidy black hair, though not what I'd call a style, angular face. His girlfriend or wife matches the look. Might even be his sister.

"Sorry for the overload, Mister. We're a bit nervous."

He glances around the room.

"You can prob'ly tell. Never been here before is all, and Val gets a bit antsy in new places. Thinking folk'll judge us... y'know... foreigners from God's Own Country..."

If I was supposed to listen rather than talk this seemed the perfect opportunity. I think the last thing he said was meant as a joke.

"New theatre?"

"Everyman."

I shake my head that no, I haven't been recently. Hard to think of it as new, even now. An awkward silence follows, so I break it.

"I can't quite place your accent?"

I don't really care but the silence was getting louder.

"Leeds... Chapeltown. You know it?"

I shake my head.

"Friend of ours from there got us the gig... we wanted a fresh start... settle down somewhere new, place going up in the world, where we can start a family..."

She nudges him in a mixture of flirtation and embarrassment, and I see the ring on her finger that confirms their status. I nod my head sagely, though going up in the World might be a false dawn, I don't want to ruin their hope just for the sake of it. I realise I still have my hat on, and slip it off as subtly as I can. I'm not sure but think men used to take their hats off inside, in the company of women.

They talk easily, and a lot, and I try to listen. Something about one of the actors getting stuck to a freshly varnished chair, a little about the flat they're renting, which is on the edge of my old stomping ground, not far from here. Not much, but a start they said. And everyone was very friendly. The neighbours they meant. They'd scouted flats with their friend, who was originally from the area, and had got a good deal. It was very like Leeds. And very different. John is wearing his only suit as they're due to go to a club later and don't know how formal it might be. But Phylis (whoever Phylis was) had mentioned that they (whoever they were) often met here first, in Ye Cracke (pronounced wrongly). I tell you all this as it unloads towards me although I can't see anything of interest or relevance in their words. I sit smiling blandly as they finish each other's sentences, in the hope of a nugget of hearing something that might be of use to me. They are clearly in the early bloom of love and devotion, but despite that, they aren't bad company, and their presence and conversation helps me fit a bit better, rather than just being a sad old soak on his own. Strange how that feels good this time around.

I can't tell you what else they talked about next, as I zone out to be honest, lost in planning out my next move. The leather jacketed Svengali in The Cali had said it wasn't about me, and not to try, that it wouldn't do me any good to think that way. I doubted listening to these two rabbit on was a likely reason for me to be here, so my present situation was of limited use. Was my task perhaps less literal than I was interpreting? Was I just supposed to listen more in general? But what would that have to do with me dying? I wanted to look around some more. If it isn't worth me trying to achieve anything specific, I may as well put myself in the path of fate, and also try out my underlying desire to meet someone a bit famous. I could wander round and see if any of the minor celebrities I'd hoped for were evident, even though I know in my heart of hearts I have no idea how to identify them even if they are here, unless they announce their name and claim to fame in my vicinity. If I did manage to find a minor celeb, I could still do what the guy in the coat wanted, and listen to someone, but hopefully with something more interesting to say than these two. Hopefully discover an unexpected revelation.

I wouldn't put it past the sarcastic cunt to mean something like that. Just before you die, you'll realise you should have listened more. It's not up there with the greatest epiphanies though, is it. And what is the death thing really all about? Try as I might to ignore the prediction, those words still haunted me on and off. The very specific details, seemingly tied to his advice for what I needed to do. Was I supposed to have listened to the phone call more closely before I went out drinking? Had I missed an important detail there? As I still can't recall a single thing about that conversation beyond the fact it happened, and I had a bad reaction to it, I doubt this.

I notice John's raised eyebrow and zone myself back to the sound of his wife's whispered voice.

"He's miles away... shall we just go?"

It's a very soft and gentle tone of voice, and she looks concerned about me. I treat them to one of my best smiles. Not great, but it's all I have.

"Sorry... something you said about..." I search my brain, grasping "...the club you were going to. Round the corner you said... do you mean the Nigerian?"

Both looks were blank in response.

"Is that a nickname? Phylis said it was called the 'Sink'? If it's a nickname that would be good to know. Details like that help you blend in..."

I apologise and say I was mistaken, blaming my age. They accept that excuse far too fucking easily. I forgive them though, as John visits the bar, and offers me a refill first. I try to keep talking to them, but it's difficult as I have no idea what they're talking about most of the time, apart from a whispered mention of 'The Beatles', as though saying the name out loud will give away a secret. If they wanted to make friends, they should just have said it loudly. "Did the Beatles drink here?" I'm sure there would be a dozen blokes in the pub who would be happy to claim early membership of the band, or close ties to one or more of the members. And to talk about it. Some of their yarns might even be vaguely true. I excuse myself to use the bathroom, hoping they'll lose interest while I'm gone.

I'm even more fortunate than that. As I come back out and stand in the doorway to the loos I can see that one of their expected friends has arrived, a young black man in a blue suit and very shiny shoes. It seems he's well known here, judging by the number of people who wave greetings at him or stop to speak. He has one of those faces that make you think you know him, and he seems vaguely familiar even to me, though there's no way I can have met him before. He squeezes onto the bench I was previously occupying, still leaving just enough room for me. I plaster on a smile and return to the table, going through the elaborate dance of distancing myself. It's almost like a script. No-one wants to be any trouble, I don't want to intrude, it was lovely for everyone to have met everyone, including Degs (the name of the new arrival) but I'll leave them in peace. I should join them at the R and B club. No, really, I should, it would be no bother and... all sorts go there. The blush on Val's face confirms this is another reference to my age. I smile weakly as I move off. I'm willing to listen to things being said as that is the task I've been set, but this was verging on the making of friends, and I really can't be arsed with that. And while the two of them have been just about bearable, acceptably self-effacing and drink-buying, this new bloke, Degs, clearly thinks of himself as the life and soul who is also going to be the centre of attention for the foreseeable. I've also taken against him. It might have been the sheen of his highly polished shoes, but I get the impression he's just the kind of poser I couldn't abide for long. There's an unknowable expression in his dark brown eyes too, like whatever is hidden beneath is quite different to the public persona. I can't shake that feeling we've met either, and that unnerves me.

I can hardly hover after I stood up, so I shuffle into the lounge, taking a stool by the bar with what remains of my pint, lighting another Pall Mall, which tastes a touch better than the previous ones, and set to listening to what is being said here. It might be what I need to hear.

#

It's a short walk of only a few hundred yards and I huddle into my coat as it's bloody freezing. I keep expecting snow, but the weather remains typically unromantic and unpleasant. Huffing to myself, I shuffle a little faster, exasperated that whatever is supposed to be happening here clearly wasn't happening in the last pub, and I feel like a character on an endless rather than straightforward quest. Rather than the simple narrative of those choose your own adventure books, this is turning out to be more like the online computer game version all the kids would play a couple of decades later, and I'm being sent on pointless tasks that never seem to end or make any sense. I find myself wondering if any boars will emerge from the side streets so I can kill ten, or there will be a series of magical bushes for me to gather prickly pears from, then find a quest giver in a long leather coat who'll explain everything as a reward. If you don't understand that analogy then fuck you. It makes sense to me. Told you, I know computers. Again, reality has refused to play ball and aside from a couple of shifty looking tramps there's nothing out of the ordinary on this journey either. On this minor backstreet I could be in almost any time period, the Anglican cathedral behind me looking complete from this angle, the half-finished Catholic one blocked by buildings ahead. It's almost like I'm outside of time.

I come to the junction of Hardman Street, which is one of the few round these particular roads that seems to have changed a fair bit, though it's reassuring that the landmarks I knew from my youth are still there. I check hopefully to my right, as one of the few other facts that I have of Liverpool's influential locations around the mid-sixties is that the corner building should be O'Connors Tavern, another legendary haunt of the Liverpool poets and the arty scene. And one additional pint won't hurt. Or a whisky. Of all the minor celebs I might see, I at least knew the fairly distinctive faces of Roger McGough, Adrian Henri and Brian Patten, the most famous poets of the day, and they went to O'Connors. If I can spot them, I can at least soak in some history being made, get drunk with them. Even if it is in a dream. But of course, the building is just a fucking Estate Agents, why would this reality do me any favours? Must have got my years wrong.

With a heavy sigh, I cross the road. I can't see my destination of the Rumblin Tum Coffee Bar standing out until I get closer, just the big writing declaring number 45, the 'Sink Club'. I'd asked someone about it before I'd left Ye Cracke, and having had it described, had realised what and where it must be. I've known this place under several names over the years, but save for the writing, it doesn't look like much has ever been structurally changed, and I walk straight in, heading down the stairs, coughing despite myself at the now expected fog of cigarette smoke wafting up.

The tobacco haze is visibly just below standing eye height round where everyone is sitting. It's loud, being quite a confined place, with three jazz musicians crowded together on the compact stage. I say jazz, as I assumed that was what the cacophony was. They might just as well been bad musicians trying to play together for the first time and each picking a different tune. Or maybe it's supposed to sound like that.

Chiding myself for reaching the age where the volume and the strangeness of the 'modern music' bother me, I aim for the snack bar. Inside, a small part of me chuckles that this is the 'modern music,' and wonders how the patron's would take to some grime, or drum n bass. Surprisingly well probably, the young are adaptable. The feel of a coffee in my hand, in the absence of a proper bar again, makes me feel more settled and I search for a spot where I can locate myself and take in the sights. I'm probably the oldest person in here, but not by much, and I'm quite surprised by the diversity of the clientele, in terms of age and of fashion; there are French crew neck sweaters alongside shirts and ties, comb-backs next to the proto ket-wig locals, and a lot of sweat.

One figure does stand out in the crowd as I looked all over the room. Round faced, round glasses, neatly trimmed goatee beard and a black shirt with some form of cravat. It rings a bell, and a thrill passes through me as I watch the figure by the stage in profile. Something seems just a fraction off. The look is certainly that of the poet Adrian Henri, but the face isn't. I say that the 'look' is that of

Adrian Henri, but it's more of a pastiche of that look. I wonder if this bloke will actually inspire the fashion I know, and Henri was the one getting it wrong? I'm tempted to squeeze my way through, past the dancefloor, to where he's sat, for a closer look, but I don't have the energy and am not all that interested once I realise he isn't the real thing. Instead, I lower myself onto one of the seats by the wall and soak up the ambience. There's a hum of voices and, strange as it seems to say, almost a vibe of happiness and freedom.

The noise (I refuse to call it music) stops quite abruptly to a smattering of half-hearted applause, and I'm jostled by a figure who apologises, then gives me a friendly grin. The one called Degs, which means that the questionable joys of John and Val won't be far behind. I nod grudgingly to the seat next to me but in a mummer's show he politely declines, indicating a group he was moving on to join. I'm glad. There's something about him I like less and less. Neither of us shouts and the conversation in the place has increased since the musicians stopped, so we complete the back and forth of nods and shrugs to convey that we understand one another. I follow his progress as he moves away and almost complete a double take when I see where he's making his way to.

The table halfway to the stage on the other side of the room has a variety of faces around it, black, white, and shades in between, but one of the faces strikes me instantly as being very familiar. I know the cheekbones well, and not just from her own face. She pulls on a cigarette and pats her swollen belly over her kaftan-like blouse with a laugh to the man next to her. I swallow hard and reached for my own cigarette. I'm almost certain.

Although speaking to him will be a physical impossibility, I think I know in my bones that Brian is very close to me, or at least what would become Brian is in the room with me. I work it through. The dates seem right, and I think I even remember the yellow and red fabric of her frock, though that could be my imagination; Sandra Touré. I always remember her as a very stern, tough lady as I've said before, strict with her son but sometimes indulgent of me, knowing I would always look out for her boy. But still scary. Well scary. Sharp-tongued. Quick to anger. I can't remember her ever actually laughing. And yet here she is, smoking, pregnant, giggling flirtatiously, and currently accepting a not very proper kiss full on the mouth from Degs, to the surprise of nobody at the table.

I hadn't seen the Leeds couple come in, or go past me, being distracted as I was, but they were now welcomed raucously by the group I'm watching, and they squeeze into the small space around the table. After a few words between them, and thinking I couldn't be any more surprised, I watch the pregnant Mrs Touré quite willingly accepting something I suspect is ill-advised into her coffee from John's concealed hip flask. I can't hear the conversation from here but Valerie is blushing and looking unhappy, and I assume is being told to relax as the hip flask empties into other coffee cups, and then directly into John's mouth.

Times change, but the knowledge from the modern age has stayed within me, and one part of that more informed self wants to march over and challenge the young lady on what she thinks she's doing, smoking and drinking when she's pregnant. Young Lady? It's too strange to see her like this. Easily thirty years my senior, and dead now of course. That's a depressing thought. But my eyes never leave her. I want to warn her, but what can I say; don't you care about your baby? (I know she did) He could be damaged in the womb? (he hadn't been). Even if I'd had the ability and bad sense to go and intervene, another part of me wouldn't want to change this amazing sight of that wonderful woman, happy and smiling and carefree for once. Reminding me so much of her son.

I scan the figures next to her to try and spot where Brian's dad might be. I'd never met him that I recall, and he was gone before I was old enough to think about it, but none of the figures look like they could be him, no West-African type features in the right age range. When you grow up in a mixed community like Toxteth, you soon get to recognise certain facial types, particularly when there are tensions between some of the communities, and there are no likely candidates for Mr Touré there, which is interesting in itself. In the sixties and in her condition, she shouldn't be sharing the company of other men in the absence of her husband, and definitely shouldn't be accepting kisses like the one from the already dislikeable Degs. I want to go over but I'm frozen. Scared. This is someone I know and... is this what I'm meant to know or do? If it finally is the reason I'm here, then I'm not sure I'm up to the job. I take a deep drag of my cigarette and force my eyes away from the table, as the beat of a Wilson Pickett song floats over the PA and the dancefloor starts to fill.

What was it he'd said, back in The Caledonia? "You can't change anything..." "You can't stop it...." And what can I change anyway in a dream? "Try listening". To what exactly? There isn't anything I can do. Am I already too late? Was there a point I've already missed which would have mattered? Mrs Touré is the closest thing to a clue I've had to finding some way I can have a role to play here. Would it have made any difference if I'd stayed and listened when the ostentatious and louche Degs had been talking in the last pub? "It isn't a linear outcome". I remember that line. So what the fuck is the point? I doubt it takes more than a few seconds for all those thoughts to push for prominence in my head. Despite the coffee I'm drinking, most of the evening has been spent with alcohol, and there's enough in me to take away my ability to grasp or hold on to logic any more.

I notice John is waving at me, and enthusiastically beckoning, clearly in the latter stages of gin happiness himself. I rise unsteadily and make my way over without thinking, keeping my eyes on John and Val as I don't want to confuse myself any more by looking at the woman who keeps calling for my attention. I have the sensation of being watched myself and it's creeping me out as I stand awkwardly in front of their table, acknowledging introductions as they're made with a weak smile, my eyes still avoiding the one place I want to look most, especially when her name is spoken out loud.

With those obligatory introductions over, I'm instantly forgotten, except by Val, a little out of the loop herself and shuffling over to make a space, as she takes pity on me. I sit gratefully, but we don't speak. You'd need to shout to do that, and we don't really have anything to say. My eyeline gradually lifts as I attempt to figure out the inter-relationships of those around me. I'm listening to the conversation but it's all music and in-jokes, and nothing that explains to me why Sandra Touré, pregnant with my unborn friend, is out of a Saturday night without her husband, in the quite cosy companionship of another man.

It had never occurred to me before, to find out exactly when Brian's father had left, he might even be out of the picture already. Shit, I hadn't thought of that, that the husband might not even be the father. No, there was a resemblance, to the photograph I'd once seen, I'm sure there was a distinctive resemblance. I think there was. A hundred options race around, pushing each other out of the way, every one of them plausible to a drunken brain. But if Brian's dad hasn't left his mum already, then he will soon. I never knew why but this could be the reason. I knew next to nothing about Mr Touré, except that he'd worked somewhere on the docks. The difficulty with getting lost in thought is that you don't pay attention to anything, including yourself. And quieted chatter around the table makes me aware I'm now staring obviously, directly and very intently at Sandra's bump, and possibly have been for some time. A track by the Dave Clarke Five is playing and that's all I can hear. And my eyes still haven't moved.

You left me High and Dry (yeah yeah)... And broken hearted (yeah yeah)

A number of other eyes are on me now, and Sandra Touré's are among them, as she shifts uncomfortably under my somewhat intense gaze. It's clear to them that something very odd is happening with me, though none of them could possibly know what it was.

We simply parted, and that was all, yep, I knew it all the time... (Yeah, yeah, yeah, Yeah, yeah, yeah)

"Hey... y'er being rude... hey, Mister... whatever your name is... hey, eyes up here..."

That's the 'chivalrous' twat Degs, loud enough to be heard over the music. I ignore him, but I do look up from the Brian bump, and directly into the eyes I remember as being hard and glassy, judgemental, resentful. My tone is flat, emotionless, but my accent is intruding into it quite clearly.

"You live on Selbourne Street, don't you? By the corner of Granby Street... first floor flat? I forget your husband's name..."

I knew the details inside out, I'd been there so many times. I didn't mean to say it and didn't even know where I was going with it, so my speech trails off. Whether she sees a recognition in me, whether the fact I know her means that I know where her family home is, and who should be there, or whether it's just the effect of a weird old man staring at her, and then saying her address out loud I don't know. But the smile is gone from her face. Despite the music there's a heavy silence around the table. Degs has a murderous expression on his face, and I may have hit upon a nerve, and am certainly ruining the plans he clearly has for the evening at the very least. No-one else knows quite what's happening, except that something very strange has just occurred, that I'm the cause, and that one of their own had been the subject and recipient. I haven't said anything offensive, and my staring might have been strange or even rude, but I hadn't been threatening. Everyone could tell that something was very wrong.

I don't say any more and am continuing to look at her, eyes unmoving. Can't help myself. Hoping for something back, some hint or recognition. Something I can listen to, like I'm supposed to. The moment hangs there.

Until she quickly gets to her feet, grabs her bag and pushes past those sat around the table, half apologising as she moves faster and faster towards the exit, almost running by the time she reaches the door. She avoids my eyes with every movement she makes, like I know something she doesn't want me to know, or doesn't want me to see how hard she's shaken by me. The shiny blue suit rises almost as soon as she does, giving me look like thunder, pausing and slowly reaching into his pocket as he faces me, his previously smiling face a mask of genuine threat. But catching a glance at how fast she's moving, he snarls once at me and turns, following after Sandra Touré, calling out her first name to no response.

It's uncomfortable at the table after that. He'd told me that there was "no point in overthinking" so I hadn't. The bastard gave shit advice, and any chance I had of learning or changing anything had just left along with the woman I'd seemingly freaked out.

"I think you should probably leave now..."

The previously retiring Valerie was the one to say it. Calmly but very firmly. More sense and nerve than any of them. I liked her. It prompted almost an epiphany in me. I genuinely didn't care that they noticed, or that they wanted me to leave. At that moment, I didn't care at all. About anything. And that is such a relief. That moment of total freedom. It was what I'd always wanted.

As I get up to take my leave, without a word of goodbye, I see the hipster by the stage with the goatee beard and round glasses watching me very closely. He's been joined by a brunette, also in glasses, very pretty smile. Almost in unison they nod at me slowly. Not in recognition, and not as though they have any idea that they know who I am. Just that I stand out as not belonging. I'm reminded of the creepy twins in The Shining. But I don't care enough to give it a second thought, I don't care about anything.

#

The cold air hitting me as I exit takes my breath away, and that sense of wonderful almost serenity I'd briefly had, goes with it. I take a deep gulp of the freezing night air and it's horrifically sobering. As is the suspicion I just came very close to being stabbed, which makes my heart pound again. I need another drink to calm me. I've been without a real drink far too long and that isn't good for me tonight. I'm not sure where to go next, not wanting to head into Town again, and my memories of the last time I'd tried to head to the Nigerian Club floating in the shadows of my brain. That choice hadn't ended well for me in 1994 and I'm currently very aware of my own mortality.

I breathe slowly and review all my conversations from earlier in the evening, trying to focus on my seeming quest, and something one of the locals in Yates's had mentioned was to do with a club, on Parliament Street on the edge of Toxteth, the "Lucky" I think he'd called it. Servicemen's club. 'The Sink' had drained the last of my hope of fulfilling any mystery mission, or I'd fucked it up already. Either way, "Lucky" seemed appropriate as I'm in need of some of that, so I aim myself back down the street I'd arrived along, stopping briefly in a pub I knew on the right called 'The Grapes', very aware it must be almost closing time, and of the need for a large whisky to keep me going, bring my heart rate back down and kick-start my alcohol stream again. I speak to no-one but the barman, order a straight treble, stand by the bar, and am ignored by all as the man serving rings the bell for last orders. I hold the glass in my hand, staring into the amber liquid.

I don't know why fate chooses that exact moment to hit me with it, but I know about that phone call at the beginning of the evening, and I know why she'd phoned me. It hits me like a sledgehammer and I forget recent events. Shelly is sick. That had been the reason for her call.

More than sick. I remember. I remember her telling me, though I hadn't understood a lot of the detail. She should have paused, let me take it in before carrying on but she hadn't. I'd heard the term "Creutzfeld-Jacob" but when she said the words, I'd joked about whether it was a new form of cracker for cheese. I'd known it was nothing like that, but it had come out of the blue and I hadn't known how to react. She hadn't taken offence, she knew my ways, but had quite calmly explain what she meant. Very little of it had gone in.

"Like my Nan, do you remember?"

I did remember. We'd taken a short weekend break to Bradford not long before we got married, in part to break the news of the upcoming happy day. Nan and Grandad Oddy were the last of Shelly's living relatives. I think she was fond of them rather than close to them, but felt an obligation to introduce the future of their genetic line. Shelly's mum had been an only child, and hadn't survived childbirth. I don't think the Oddy's had ever forgiven Liverpool for that. And it had seemed to me they weren't impressed by me much either. I'll admit now I wasn't the type to charm people on first meeting, I'm more of an acquired taste if I'm honest, and I'd gone to please her rather than from any real desire to meet future relatives. I'd been thinking of that holiday earlier tonight while she told me the further details of her own illness, her voice soft, low, and calm. Her own fault, she'd brought her family up in the conversation.

The fact I'd had to sleep on the couch hadn't endeared them to me any further, nor the barely disguised disappointment that she was marrying someone like me. The dislike and uneasy attempts at civility had been mutual. She told me when we'd arrived back home that it wasn't like that at all, that they were genuinely pleased, just not used to outsiders when they'd had news of their own to break. I hadn't been in the room when they told her, I'd found out in the pub later that evening that Nan had this Creutzfeld thing. We hadn't had the internet back then and didn't need to know the gory details anyway, beyond the fact it was terminal and that her immediate life expectancy wasn't good. I'd tried to warm to them when we got back from the pub because that's what you do, but whether they were just as uncomfortable with me knowing as I was in the knowledge, I wasn't sure, but we'd only stayed one more night, and had then left to come back to Liverpool and give them some peace. My idea. They hadn't travelled for the wedding. Nan was too ill, though as religious folk I doubt they'd have been happy attending a registry office service anyway. Grandad Oddy didn't live much longer than his wife, though he at least lasted until after our daughter's birth. Never met her though. We were due to visit him a few months afterwards but a heart attack took him too.

I'm still nursing the large whisky, lost in those details I've been trying so hard to remember, and those which I'd forgotten years earlier. I can't even picture what they looked like, beyond 'old'. I drain the glass in one and indicate I want another before the final bell. Things are cheap in this time.

"Don't worry, I'll be fine and I don't need you to do anything for me. I have people…"

I pull myself back to that phone call itself. That sentence had been the one which first made me reach for my whisky bottle. Some vestiges of guilt might have been present I suppose, that she'd been there for me in my own life-threatening illness, but I ignored that and chose to take offence instead. Why would I want to be there for her? Do anything for her? She couldn't just phone up out of the blue and expect me to drop everything and come running just because she was ill. And what did "I have people" mean? Was she telling me she'd found someone new, the insensitive bitch? I don't think I'd said anything back, but she may have heard the screw cap being undone.

"I'm not sad or angry, it just happens sometimes… you know that…"

She'd started telling me what the disease was, what it meant, what her prognosis was. I'd zoned it all out, not wanting to know and wishing she hadn't phoned at all. It would have been kinder to just die and let me find out later. I hadn't bothered with a glass. It would just have added an unnecessary step from the bottle to my mouth. I don't know how long she'd talked without me saying anything but eventually she'd either noticed, or felt compelled to raise the fact in that fucking gentle, calm voice she seemed to have channelled. It was fucking spooky. I'd told her as much and she ignored the barb.

"It's a shock, I know..."

The shock was that she expected me to care. But I'm so dumb I hadn't seen the sucker punch coming.

"But... we have to talk about Sarah... I haven't told her yet..."

It took a moment for that to sink in. I don't know if she'd mentioned Bradford to ease me into thoughts of last living relatives, but that was where I now felt it. The underhanded bitch. Couldn't guilt me. And it was a bit fucking late for me to start being a father now. The years that might have mattered had passed. I'd slugged more whisky, starting to get angry.

Why had I got angry?

#

It was freezing outside the pub again, but freshly fortified and forcing myself to think that my regained memory was some type of success I hardly notice, just pulling my jacket tighter once more, for all the good it does, and accepting the drizzle which had started to come down as typical of my fortunes. The details of the phone call don't matter, do they? I look down at my non-existent watch. Had I just remembered because my predicted time is about to be up, was that what this whole thing was about? Time to remember, and return to reality? The rain is coming down harder. At least I have a hat, there are some positives out of being dressed like this. I'd asked where the 'Lucky' club was before I'd left the pub and the barman hadn't known, but someone sat by the door had told me. I'd paid no attention to who, and didn't bother to thank them for the information. It had been a long day and the last thing I wanted was any more conversation or listening. Live in the moment. That had been his other advice.

The Cathedral looks beautiful in the moonlight, even the clouds add rather than take away from the view. The new boxy housing estate which will be at the rear of the site hasn't been built yet, and this makes the picture very different. I'm tempted to walk through the graveyard below, revisit where all this started, so long ago. So long ago now, sitting in the Caledonia. When I wake, in my flat, if I wake there, it will only have been a couple of hours before now in real time. For me here, it's almost two days ago. I wonder what will happen when I finally get back, if I'll remember all this. And momentarily, just momentarily, I wonder if I will return at all. And if I want to.

I'm not 100% convinced my interpretation of returned memories being due to the end of this predicted life is correct. If truth be told, I'm starting to doubt everything again. The amount of whisky I've just quickly consumed doesn't help, plus the build up of the booze from over the last few hours. I question the truth of everything, and logic and fact blur through the alcohol. I had been desperate for some kind of sign about Brian, and had fixated on a young woman, who was nothing like Mrs Touré in manner or behaviour, had convinced myself it must be her, and that her being in the same club as me was a sign. Had I just imagined her name being said? Realistically, it's more likely I've just scared the shit out of a total stranger, my wish fulfilment fucking up a perfectly nice evening for her and her likely boyfriend, and father of her unborn child. And I'd quite possibly almost been stabbed because of it. I'm such a prick. If I can't trust what I'd been sure of so recently, how can I trust anything else I believe to be true?

If the predictions of my two harbingers of doom were correct, then my time here must be literally almost up, though whether that is meant to mean that my time (and death) is here in 1964, or back in the present day I don't know. It's the kind of thing I really should have asked, come to think about it. But either way I'll be glad when it's finally over. Everything. I'm so tired.

I turn left for a detour, in order to stand by the railings and look down into St James' Gardens, and the vista in front of me is startling. It's full of graves. Absolutely full of graves. The fact there are graves in the graveyard doesn't surprise me, I'm not that stupid, but it has long since been landscaped into a park, the 'Lost Boys' garden as it's known, with the grave markers from the orphanage propped up to line the boundaries, the remaining tombstones gathered and re-laid in what I guess is meant to be a more pleasing aesthetic, with plenty of green space. I assume the bodies beneath have been re-interred elsewhere. Seeing so many tombs right now is a shock.

"Brian..." I can hear his name echo in my head, and can't make it stop.

"You can't save him either..."

Too much death. Something so familiar is so different, even after all I've seen the past hours, and a part of my brain had been considering going back down to the park bench I'd originally woken up on in 1994, and falling asleep there. Make things nice and neat and cyclical. But the tombs make me pause.

I can't stop the floodgates of memory from opening, things I've been searching so hard for come like an unstoppable torrent.

I hadn't held back when Shelly had said we needed to talk about our child. I hadn't answered her repeated and quite reasonable questions and pleas for re-assurance about Sarah. It had seemed like she was trying to make me promise to be a father to our daughter, to take her on, as if I was in any state to do that. Like she wouldn't find a way to blame me for her mother's death too. I'd shouted down the phone until I was hoarse, breaking only to take down more whisky, and she'd just accepted and taken it, letting me wear myself out. Such vitriol. I'd been waiting for her to mention my drinking, and to tell me it wasn't a good idea. Waiting, so I would have had another reason to scream at her some more. She'd done that once before. Shelly's father had done a good job in raising her on his own, at a time when that kind of parenting wasn't the norm, but he'd balanced it out with an increase in his own alcoholism. Not like me, he didn't drink in a pub, he hadn't been in one since the death of his wife and Shelly's birth. All the same the booze left him dead at fifty. Cirrhosis. It had been when she was caring for me after the cancer. She'd told me then that she didn't wanted to lose me the same way she'd lost her dad. Had wanted me to take better care of myself. I'd told her to fuck off. She'd got so upset and ended up screaming at me that I was a selfish bastard and that she wanted me to live, even if I didn't. I'd wanted her

214

to say it again on the phone call, so I could tell her to fuck off and slam the phone down. Or whatever the equivalent is on a mobile.

She hadn't said a word about my drinking, but had played the guilt card about Sarah being alone, having no-one. She'd got a little angrier as the call went on longer and longer, the tables turning so it was her turn to get frustrated and tell me this wasn't how she'd wanted the conversation to go at all. And then she had started shouting back at me. That had been easier. In the end she'd almost screamed at me that it was my responsibility, it didn't matter what I wanted, having a child meant you had responsibilities. And the consequence was I was going to be our daughter's last living relative, and she'd need someone. I had to live with that, because she couldn't. I put this together now with the revelation she was carrying a child herself, but she hadn't told me that. I'd refused to engage any more when it reached that point, and had switched my phone off in the middle of her sentence. I refused to be drawn into things that didn't concern me. I didn't want any of it.

The rain is coming down even faster now, and I'm still looking over the railings and into the cemetery. The sight and reminder of so much death prompts a sudden sensation of vomit rising into my gullet. It rises more and I actually retch, but nothing comes up. A couple of cars drive past, seeing an old soak, maybe homeless, simply being sick after drink, which would be what he did. They drive on. I fumble for my last but one cigarette and light it, stumbling back away from a sight I hated, and towards the more hopeful view of the Cathedral. I force everything but the here and now back out of my aching brain. Live in the moment. I cling to the command.

#

I pay attention to everything though my vision is starting to blur, I want to block out the voices and thoughts and just focus on the here and now, while I still can. At the far end I know there are elements of the imposing structure yet to be built, but it looks pretty complete to me. On the right are a row of decrepit tenements, soon for demolition I guess. In the distance, a few figures are moving this way and that. I squint through the rain, thinking one might have a peaked cap, next to another in a long leather coat, but it could be my imagination. My nerves are shot, and I have to admit I'm not just slightly drunk, not even close. Dry retching had the result of making me feel it all the more, rather than less. I'm totally fucked up. The whiskies and retching have re-animated the sloshing of beer still in my belly.

Which has miraculously just stayed put when, if there was any justice in the world, it should have been all over the pavement.

I hurry onwards, now changing my mind and deciding to pay as little attention as possible to my surroundings as they are doing to me. Fuck the predictions and advice. Fuck everything. Fuck Shelly, fuck Sarah, fuck Brian. The good thing about being pissed is that you can change your view and decisions instantly, without feeling like you're being inconsistent or hypocritical. Even if you don't mean a word of it. I persuade myself this is living in the moment too, just a different aspect to it. Doing what the fuck I please, minute by minute.

I soon reach the steep border of Upper Parliament Street, the divider from Toxteth and where I really belong. A row of Georgian houses lines the far side, and to my left I know were the clubs I'm more familiar with but over the road, and almost opposite me, I can just make out the word 'Lucky Bar' under an awning, part way along the terrace.

"Lucky, fucking lucky... what second chance you cunt? what was I supposed to have done differently? What the fuck was it and did I do it...? Was it her? Oh, who gives a fuck..."

I'm barely aware of the words that I mumble while I squint up and down the street, checking for potentially lethal traffic, still finding it unexpectedly busy for this late at night. I like it that I can still be surprised. In one segment of my mind, even though I had been alive in '64, this was 'the past' so should be all cobbled streets, trams and horse-drawn carriages. In another part I think I know who the man with the limp was now, that it hadn't just been a dalliance with Sandra, but I can't find the energy to care.

"Who gives a fuck?" I shout it at the road and cars and at nothing and no-one in particular, feeling a cathartic release. A primal scream of getting that out of me and challenging the World to argue. It doesn't, but I know they're just words and I don't mean them. I'm going to die, my wife is going to die, all my family, and there's nothing I can do to stop it. I've given up hope of that. Except Brian. Even though he's already long dead, he's the one I still want to be able to save.

I am only vaguely aware of the other voices at first. There is a stream of traffic driving past, karma for my blasphemy so close to a house of God, and that logic intrudes insidiously into my thoughts, rambling, shouting and musings as I wait for a gap in the cars. The thought of karma draws my attention to the sound of an accent I think I recognise.

"Is that the bastard... are you sure?"

I don't hear the response, but I don't even bother to look round either. I know they're here for me. I don't care how he'd found me, or that he'd brought friends. I just accept that it doesn't matter what I do or say now, doesn't matter what I said or did earlier. I wonder absently which of them got to me first. The final words I hear clearly are whispered and carried on the wind.

"Butterflies, Jack... dozens of them... aren't they pretty?"

The indistinct voices spit out anger from behind me as the cars carry on past in a steady stream, not showing any signs of slowing, caring, or allowing me an option of crossing. I feel a peace settle over me. I don't turn round. I feel a hand grab my shoulder roughly as a mouth almost pressed up against my ear, spittle flecking my cheek.

"Hey nigger lover... remember me?"

FIVE – 18th October

From your perspective, you can see a man sitting silently on a park bench, staring into nothingness, waiting. The smell of engine oil drifts lazily across his nostrils as children play, only a few yards away. A raindrop bounces off the peak of the man's hat. He has no reason to react. No place he needs to be. His job is done.

#

In another place, a grandchild gurgles happily, fist clenching onto an old and creased black finger. The finger is part of a body that has lived a full and hard life. The body belongs to a man who is content. He's raised a family the same way that his own parents did, with love but a firm set of morals. Occasionally a necessary spanking, but not one that was never resented afterwards. Accepting his children's choices, but guiding where he could. His daughter will do the same for hers, he's sure of that. There's something about the thin lips of the happy ball of blue-eyed child that reminds him of someone, though he can't place who. That picture fades.

#

You can see a pint of bitter, placed on a beermat, resting on a large square table set next to the big French windows of the pub, the view looking out over the park and the leafy suburbs of Liverpool. Next to it, on its own beermat, is a smaller glass with a double measure of spirits. An empty tonic bottle.

Sat at the end of the table is a tired looking woman, short tidy hair, green eyes. She looks exhausted but not unhappy as she stares out of the windows, at the green grass and shedding trees, mostly bare by now. It is late afternoon, dusk hovering beyond the cluster of trees, waiting behind a fluffy cloud.

If she's waiting for something or someone, she doesn't seem too perturbed by the delay. Her eyes slowly scan over to the table and drinks. Her hand extends, first towards the pint, then to the spirits. Her expression doesn't alter as she lifts the smaller glass high, looking through the liquid as though you might a magnifying glass. She puts it against her thin mouth and pauses a moment, rolling the glass back and forth along her lower lip. She tips it and drains the liquid in a single gulp.

#

The inside of The Caledonia pub looks almost deserted. Rain hammers on the windows, and the final glasses are being collected. 'Last orders' has long since rung. The table by the window is empty, one chair pulled back as though someone has left in a hurry. A cigarette butt, stamped with someone's shoe or boot and brought in on the underside, is very noticeable on the otherwise clean floor.

There is a brilliant flash of lightning outside the window, and it seems to frame the back wall of the pub like a proscenium arch for just one moment. If you'd paid attention, you'd have noticed that the bright light seemed to spotlight the woman in the picture hanging there, and she seemed to be looking in just slightly different directions with each eye.

One seems to track the doorway leading to the toilets, and in the flash of electric brilliance, it seemed to be actively searching there. Her other eye is blankly staring straight ahead, towards the exit from the pub. She looks bored. Resigned. Unless that's just a pose.

If you were watching from another angle in that burst of illumination, you might interpret her expression differently, as one of quiet satisfaction. Not happiness, not joy, but of contentment that things are as they should be.

The light is followed by an almost deafening sound of thunder that echoes through the room.

AUTHOR NOTE – Language which may offend

I feel compelled to add a note to the end of this book. When I started writing this story, I had no idea that bigotry and prejudice of all kinds would be a major theme of the narrative, and it just emerged through the writing and research, so take that as you will, but hopefully it means that the characters took on a real life of their own, and needed their stories to be told. It's the most satisfying type of writing when the words themselves guide the story. More often than not, the direction of a story takes a lot of hard work, which accounts for the vast number of partly written novels in the World.

There are certain terms and epithets, whether religious, racial, homophobic, misogynist or misanthropic, which are uncomfortable and difficult to use in any context, as received wisdom is that people outside of certain demographics shouldn't utilise these words. I did consider using what they currently call a 'sensitivity reader' to check my drafts for how people might react, particularly in our current climate, but eventually decided against it, as the historical periods I'm writing about wouldn't have had that option, so my characters shouldn't either. Plus, the phrases and terminology used in the story are just words, tools, and this is a piece of fiction. One of my personal beliefs is that by demonising terms and making actual words taboo we inadvertently give them, return to them, or intensify in them, a power they shouldn't have as a string of alphanumeric characters placed in a certain order. Some take the view that by ignoring or avoiding certain words, or adding an asterisk (a pet hate of mine, as though the spelling itself is also offensive, but less so if you miss out a vowel) it's possible to avoid offence, but for me it just exacerbates and prolongs problems, blaming vocal and written expressions for intent, attitudes, actions and prejudice when it should be the other way around.

If I may be allowed to preach for a moment longer (non-denominationally, and as a devout atheist), prejudice isn't the Candyman; you don't say a particular word several times and it then appears. Prejudice is here with or without certain iconography and lexicon, and missing that point is to be misdirected. Words aren't the instigator of prejudice, they are (or can be) the tools used to show it, but intent is too frequently sidelined when people can signal their own superiority and apparent morality more easily by jumping on terminology. I don't (and wouldn't claim) to be any expert on prejudice, and am aware I've had a privileged life, not experiencing any of the extreme abuse, or more silent but just as debilitating discrimination that others do, but I try to learn, and take a reasoned response to what I learn. Anyway, the point of this note is that I genuinely struggled with whether or not I should tone down some of the terms which are historically apposite, because some readers might find real offence in them. I eventually decided that if I did substitute less offensive terminology and insults, then I'd be untrue to the story, characters and the setting. Pretending overt discrimination and insult didn't and don't happen, especially during the sixties, but later too, is misleading. I leave it up to the reader to decide the actual motivations of the characters, and where insult was intended and where it wasn't, and for what purpose.

Having said that, if any of the terms incorporated into the dialogue have offended, I'm genuinely sorry and apologise to you.

Contact me

Thank you for reading *The Raven Sound*.

If you enjoyed my writing, why not log onto www.kitderrick.com and sign up for the newsletter to be notified when I publish something new.

Or follow me at the tweetyplace on @kitderrick1

Printed in Great Britain
by Amazon